A

Rebel

Star

By

Alyssa Rae

For Celestine,

love

Alyssa Rae

Although historical names have been used, this work is purely fiction. Names, characters, places, incidents and situations are the product of the author's imagination and are used fictitiously. References to actual persons, living or dead, business establishments, events, or locales are used fictitiously. The publisher does not have any control over and does not assume responsibility for author or third-party websites or their content.

ISBN: 978-0692504901

For Nana and Papa and all the love, laughs, and $20 bills they've given me over the years,

For Bob Caron and his constant excitement and support of my writing,

For Michael P. who found his way into the story,

For my Mom who continues to show her unfailing support and encouragement,

For my Dad who still lets me live with them for free.

Prologue

Being a survivor is overrated. Then again, so is being a martyr. But, which is better? Is staying alive to see the results of your hard work better than becoming the symbol that moves people to fight for your cause? Surviving means hard work and constant struggle. A martyr is what inspires. I've met many martyrs in my lifetime, all of them happy in life, all of them satisfied with the inspiration that followed their death. They weren't alive to see what that inspiration caused. They weren't alive to see their family or friends suffer or to watch their people burn.

I was.

Yes, to be a martyr is better. Take it from me, I'm the survivor.

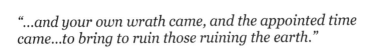

"...*and your own wrath came, and the appointed time came...to bring to ruin those ruining the earth.*"

Revelation 11:18
New World Translation of the Holy Scriptures

Chapter 1

1991

"Alright everyone, settle down. I've finally got this thing working," my teacher announced. It was my last class of the day, and I was counting the minutes until my best friend Kirstin and I could go on the shopping trip we had been planning all week. It was a Friday afternoon and my history teacher had wheeled the school's old television set into the classroom so we could watch something he recorded on the news. It took him fifteen minutes to get the VCR to work.

"Now," he said once we were quiet, "we've been studying the country of Nigeria and the affect we British have had on its history. We've learned that Nigeria has fought many civil wars to establish its current government. What I want all of you to learn and understand from the example of Nigeria is that even after a war is won a country can still struggle. We are going to listen to a speech given by one of Nigeria's most beloved writers, given only a few nights ago. I want each and every one of you to pay close attention to what he says."

Our teacher pressed the "play" button on the VCR and took his seat at his desk. The room was dark and after a few seconds of fuzziness the picture on the screen showed a room full of people and one man, standing at a podium in the front. His name was Ken Saro-Wiwa and this was the first time I heard him speak.

He addressed the audience then began:

"I wish to thank you all for the kind sentiments you have expressed here either in words or by your mere presence. It is gratifying to know that there are people who care for your ideas while you are still alive.

"A writer is his cause. At fifty, he may still dream dreams and see visions, but he must also wither into the truth. So today, I re-dedicate myself to what has always been my primary concern as a man and a writer: the development of a stable, modern Nigeria which embraces civilized values; a Nigeria where no ethnic group or individual is oppressed, a democratic nation where minority rights are protected, education is a right, freedom of speech and association are guaranteed and where merit and competence are held as beacons. Convinced that most Nigerians share this concern I will stand for it at all times and in all places.

"...What we have today is the rump of a country, illiterate, lacking in moral fiber, financially bankrupt, and tottering dangerously on the brink of disaster. This should shake us out of all complacency."

3

Ken Saro-Wiwa was a powerful and moving speaker. I was only able to understand some of what he said throughout his speech because we had barely skimmed the surface of the true political troubles in Nigeria, but I found myself listening intently to every word he said. He went on to speak about the Federation, or government, of Nigeria and how through that Federation the country had suffered and not all ethnic groups were treated equally. He continued:

"...We must end immediately the oppression of minority ethnic groups and free all Nigerians to express themselves and develop their cultures, their languages and their political systems using their resources as best they may...

"...Oil pollution is a great menace to the Nigerian environment. I wish to warn that the harm being done to the environment of the Niger River Delta must be ameliorated by the oil companies which prospect for oil there; the degradation of the ecosystem must end and

the dehumanization of the inhabitants of the areas must cease and restitution be made for past wrongs."

Several of my classmates turned to look at me while he spoke of the environmental destruction caused by the oil companies; one company in particular. My father worked at the head of a branch in one of the companies that was being accused of negligence. I, though, had nothing to do with my father's company or what it did in other countries and, even if I did, there was nothing I could have done to fix it. My father didn't like it when my brother and I asked him questions about the stories we heard about the company. He liked to keep us ignorant of the situation and the politics that went with it and, personally, I really didn't care to worry about it. Instead of being embarrassed by my classmates' accusing stares, I stuck my chin up a little higher and continued to listen to the end of Ken Saro-Wiwa's speech.

"Our ship of state is today sinking! A few are manipulating the system to their advantage, but our

intellectuals, our women, our youth, the masses are being flushed down the drain. All our systems, educational, economic, health, are in a shambles. Yet we persist in our natural obtuseness... No. As I say...to be, we have to think.

"...I call upon all the minority ethnic groups in Nigeria to follow the example of the Ogoni people and demand their rights to political autonomy and freedom in Nigeria. In times past, such minority commitment has saved Nigeria. It can be so, even now as the nation stands on the crossroads once again.

"I appeal to those friends of our country whose endeavors brought the country together in the first place and where investment and technology keep it going today to assist in this search for a rational solution to the Nigerian dilemma without placing too much of a burden on our severely distressed populace. Before the curtain falls.

"I also appeal to the Nigerian press to continue to stand courageously for a democratic Nigeria according to the wishes of all Nigerians to crusade for social justice and for the rights and liberties of the oppressed masses, oppressed ethnic groups and the disadvantaged of our country. Else the curtain will fall.

"Thank you."[1]

My teacher turned the television off and stood back up in front of the class. He asked us to write a summary of the speech over the weekend to be turned in on the following Monday. The speech took up our entire class, so by the time our teacher finished telling us our assignment, the bell rang and we were set free.

I waited for my friend Kirstin in the front of the school by the car my father sent to pick us up. She

---

[1] *See Bibliography*

arrived shortly after me, excited for our shopping day and looking better than everyone else in her school uniform. As Kirstin approached me and the car, a girl from my class shouted, "Murderers!" at both of us.

"What is her problem?" Kirstin asked sticking her nose in the air.

"We watched a video of a speech about how the oil companies are destroying the African environment," I explained.

Kirstin shrugged, "As if that's our fault. Ready to go shopping?"

"Yeah let's go." I said. Yet I couldn't help but wonder, was it our fault?

<u>Chapter 2</u>

1992

Everyone turned and applauded as I made my grand entrance to the party. My father, once again, outdid himself with the arrangements; one thing he was always good at was throwing an extravagant party. All the guests were people he considered to be the most important in London's social class, the richest of the rich who could help him further his business and career. I was wearing a light green sundress that stopped above my knees, with a large, white, floppy hat and white, strappy sandals. We were having a tea and garden party in our backyard in celebration of my graduation from high school. I walked out onto the back balcony and down the grand staircase, my hand skimming over the surface of the railing to guide me down onto the patio. Craig, my older brother by two years, was the first to greet me at the bottom of the steps.

"Congratulations, Mari!" No one ever used my full name Marienela. He picked me up and spun me around in a circle. There was light laughter from the guests who were waiting their turn to congratulate me.

"Where is Father?" I quickly whispered to Craig.

"I haven't seen him yet. Don't worry, he'll be here, he promised." He must have seen me frown because he added, "Hey, forget about him. Today is all about you."

Craig winked and stepped aside for the other guests. The first was my boyfriend Brian. Brian and Craig were close friends and attended university together. We were the perfect couple, Brian and I, the kind everyone is jealous of. Brian was the same age as my brother, a little bit taller than me, clean-cut, with black hair and brown eyes. He was the perfect complement to my light brown hair and hazel-sometimes-green eyes. His father worked for mine and an alliance between our families would result in nothing less than extreme power and wealth. Besides, both families came from old money and old money must always stick with old money.

The next person was Kirstin. Kirstin was a pretty blonde and a complete airhead. I know that sounds mean, but there is just no other way to describe her. I'm not saying that because she was blond she was dumb nor am I saying the reverse. I'm simply saying that she was a blonde. And she was dumb. She cared about nothing unless it was related to shopping and spending money, and she cared about no one except for my brother—a girlhood crush she never grew out of. Fortunately, Craig couldn't stand her. I didn't particularly like Kirstin—no one really did—and I'm certain she didn't like me. But, she was from old money and old money must always stick with old money. In other words, we were best friends.

Kirstin took the tips of my hands in hers and, careful not to lean her body too close, gave me a small peck on each cheek. "Can you believe it?" She asked in excitement. "We're finally out of school!"

"Aren't you going to University?" Brian asked wrapping an arm around my waist.

"Well yes, but that's different," she replied.

"Extremely different," Craig joined in. "There's more homework, and it's harder. The professors are great though. They give you all the time you need and never pressure you or grade you badly." The last part of his comment was sarcasm and, as usual, Kirstin did not understand it.

"See! I can't wait to start," she beamed at us. Like I said: airhead. It was a small joke between the three of us to tease Kirstin whenever possible. Brian, at times, thought it was mean, but that never stopped him from joining in. Craig liked to do it because, in his words, he enjoyed testing the limits of her stupidity. Me, I did it to keep her in her place. Kirstin was the biggest snob I knew, who believed she was better than everyone she met and was going to meet. Everyone that is, except for me. She may have come from a lot of money, but my family had more.

The rest of my party was a mixture of accepting cards and congratulations from the assortment of people my father considered important enough to invite. We sat at fancy, covered tables eating finger foods and drinking tea out of the finest china cups money could buy. There were about 100 people at the party and at some point my father finally made his appearance. He joked and laughed and gave a speech about how proud he was, even though the speech was more about him than me. All in all, things went smoothly until I noticed Joseph, our live-in cook, come outside and whisper something in my father's ear. My father smiled and thanked him, then abruptly left his guests and followed Joseph into the house.

My father not only worked for an oil company, he owned a portion of *the* oil company. This oil company was, and is, one of the biggest oil companies in the world. My father sat on the board of directors and controlled one of the largest branches of the company: the Nigerian Branch. Needless to say, he was a busy man, so when he excused himself from the party to discuss business, it was nothing out of the ordinary. Of course, that didn't stop me from following him.

I don't know if it was a premonition or some sort of sixth sense, but I knew when my father slipped away with Joseph that something important was going to happen. I had this feeling that I needed to know what he was up to, so I also excused myself from my table and followed him into the house. I knew he would be heading for the library, which doubled as his office, so I went straight in that direction. Our library was small and smelled deliciously of books. It would have been my favorite room in the house if it weren't for the large, mahogany desk that stood in the center. The desk turned the innocent room into my father's home office, making it a place we all avoided. I tip-toed towards the door and—Jackpot!—saw that he left it open a crack. I pressed my ear close and listened.

"What sort of trouble?" My father asked.

Another man's voice answered, "They are refusing to allow us to lay the pipeline through their land, sir."

"I don't care what they're refusing to do, they have no more rights to that land," my father replied.

The other man cleared his throat. I could hear the fear in his voice as he said, "Well sir, they actually do."

"Excuse me?" My father rarely raised his voice even when he was angry. He didn't need to, usually the look on his face was enough.

"The people still technically own those lands. They refused to sell and they never left even after they were...evicted."

"Simon, I'm going to lay that pipeline straight through the middle of Ogoniland whether the people like it or not."

"But sir..."

"Find me a way," my father cut him off.

I could tell the meeting was over and, not wanting to get caught, I hurried away from the door. Simon was my father's assistant at work, which is why I recognized the voice. He kept everything in order for my father while also taking care of some of his personal affairs. Simon was nice enough, but he was weak. Sure, he could keep a calendar organized and take phone messages and he worked for one of the most powerful men in London, but he was a cowering fool most of the time. No wonder I thought he sounded afraid. I almost made it all the way back to the party when I heard Father's voice behind me.

Mari?"

"Hello Father, I was just coming to find you," I acted surprised to find him coming out of the library. "Some of the guests were looking for you."

"Yes, sorry about that. I'm afraid I have to leave. Something urgent has come up at work and it cannot wait."

"So I see," I replied coolly. "I think I've become as used to you leaving as Mother was." I don't know why I mentioned my mother, but my father's entire demeanor changed when I did.

"What did you say?" He stepped towards me closing the gap between us, his face only inches from mine. "You know nothing about your mother." My courage faltered and I took a step back from him. I could see the rage in his eyes as he stood over me, but as quickly as it appeared it went away. He pulled back and tugged on his jacket to make sure it was straight.

"Please make my excuses to our guests. See if you can do something without being childish, for once."

He walked by me and out the front door. I stood there in the front of our house, alone, trying to make sense of what had happened. My father and I definitely did not have the best relationship—I'm pretty sure we despised each other equally—but he didn't often lash out at me. He usually replied with equal coolness and sarcasm. He had a special way of using his words to make people feel small. In that moment I felt six inches high, and in his words, childish. I did the only thing I knew how to do: I ran away.

I ran to my mother's old sitting room, which was the only room in the house that ever made me feel safe.

My mother spent a lot of time in her sitting room, drinking tea and reading, especially towards the end of her life. She often allowed Craig and me to sit with her, so she could read aloud to us from her favorite chair. She was always happy in that room. Whenever I wanted to think about her that is where I would go.

Her name was Lila. People tell me all the time that I look just like her. She was young with light brown hair that was streaked blonde by the sun. Her eyes were bright green and her skin was tanned with freckles. She was a teenager when she met my father, and back then he must have been much more charming because she instantly fell in love with him. He was from a wealthy, London family and she was an orphan living in a small Nigerian village. Her family was originally from England but moved to Nigeria when she was born. Her parents, my grandparents, were killed while she was still very young and instead of going back to England, a country she had never seen, Lila was taken in by a kind family who raised her in their village against the backdrop of the Niger River Delta.

It was my father that created the desire in her to leave the only home she ever knew. Their relationship developed quickly. Before she knew it, Lila was moving to London and getting married to a man she barely knew. My brother made his appearance within the first year of their marriage and then two years later, they had me. I never knew my mother when she was truly happy; by the time I was born the weight of living with a man like my father had aged her. She and Father often argued, but mostly they tried their best to avoid each other.

In the end it was the cold, London weather that killed my mother. She was a sickly person. She grew up in the hot humidity of the African jungle near the equator. The cold rain and fog of London caused her to frequently catch colds. When I was four, she caught a cold and never got better. The cold festered in her chest for months and eventually developed into pneumonia. She no longer had the will to fight and by the time I turned five, she passed away.

I used to be so angry with her for giving up that easily. Craig was devastated but found a way to forgive her for leaving us so soon. Father seemed indifferent. After Lila died, he cared for nothing else but his work. Craig and I grew used to his absence and with the help of our nanny and our cook, both of whom lived with us, we took care of ourselves.

Our nanny's name was Ruth and her brother, Joseph, was our cook. Mother hired both of them when she became sick and after she died, they moved into our house to continue taking care of us. They were also from Africa, from the Congo, and reminded her of home. They in turn cared about her so much, that they were willing to help raise her children even after she was gone and despite the fact that our Father became their boss. When Mother died, our father gave up on us. We weren't only motherless—we were orphans.

Ruth became more than a nanny to us. She was our caregiver, housekeeper, nurse, and overall guardian. She was the one who praised us when we did well and grounded us when we misbehaved, which happened often in my case. She bandaged our cuts and signed our permission forms for school. Joseph cooked all of our meals, packed our school lunches, did all of the grocery shopping, and made sure we ate healthy. He also made us laugh when we were down and took our side even when we were wrong. Craig and I never would have survived without either of them.

I entered the little yellow sitting room my mother loved so much and sat down on the floor beside her favorite chair. I was the only one who still went into her room, everyone else stayed far away from it. I could hide away in there for hours and no one would ever find me. I went there whenever I felt lonely or I missed Mother, but sometimes I went there to think.

There was a small bookshelf next to Mother's chair. I ran my hands over the books on the lower shelves, reading the titles as I went along: *Romeo & Juliet, Wuthering Heights, Jane Eyre, Anna Karenina, The Great Gatsby, Les Miserables,* and *Lorna Doone.* She read them all. These were all of her favorites, all grouped together on one little shelf. I picked up *Wuthering Heights*, which was her favorite of them all, and noticed something I never had before. There was a small, leather bound journal tucked away behind all the books. It was hidden as though it had been stashed there on purpose. I reached in the back and pulled it out.

The journal was made of brown leather, the edges of the pages were yellowed. It wasn't very old, but it was as dusty as the other books on the shelf. I carefully flipped through the pages. They were filled with thin, cursive words, written with a careful hand in black ink. The handwriting was beautiful and familiar: my mother's. I closed the journal and reopened it to the very first page. My breath caught in my throat as I read the first words.

A Rebel Star

To my children: Craig and Marienela.

I'm so sorry I couldn't stay with you. I hope this journal will be able to answer your questions. I made mistakes when I was young, mistakes that I hope you can learn from. I have written everything down, please forgive me for not being able to tell you myself. You two are the most important things in my life.

I love you so much!

Your mother,

Lila

I locked myself in my room for the rest of the afternoon and night, never returning to my party, and read every word my mother wrote to us. She began the journal while she was sick almost as if she knew all along that she was going to die. She described her life in Nigeria when she was young, before her parents died,

24

and then afterwards what it was like growing up in the village with the family that took her in. She described the beauty of her homeland and her love for it. She wrote about meeting Father and how the villagers begged her to stay away from him. *"But it was too late,"* she wrote, *"I was already in love with him."* The second half of the journal was about her life in England, living in a giant house with running water and a man she barely knew. Despite being in such a strange place she was happy. At first, it was the grand adventure she always wanted, but in the end she missed home.

The journal was a letter to me and to Craig; our mother's goodbye letter, her last words to us. There were three clear messages within its pages, three things she wanted us to know. One: our father killed her. He tricked her into leaving her home, convincing her that he loved her and telling her that he would bring her back one day. Well, he did bring her back to Nigeria, except he waited for her to die first. He didn't let Craig and me go with him, but after Mother died he took her ashes back to her home and scattered them over her favorite place. It was the only thing he ever did for her; the only promise he never broke. Two: he was destroying her home. When they met, Father was on a business trip in Nigeria. He was young and just beginning his career in the oil company. He took a risk and volunteered to travel to Nigeria to open a new branch for the company. He was there to oversee the opening and to collect samples from the surrounding areas. My mother's village was sitting on top of some of the richest oil in the Niger River Delta and he wanted it. I immediately recognized the name of the place where Mother was from: Ogoniland. The same place I heard Father arguing about during my party. Whatever was going on at the company branch in Nigeria it had to do with my Mother's village. Three: she wanted Craig and me to go to Nigeria. She didn't say it directly, but she wanted her children to see her home, the place she loved so much. I made a promise to myself and to my mother before I went to sleep that night. I promised that, no matter what, I would find my way to Ogoniland one day and I would drag Craig along with me.

Chapter 3

Kirstin and I often met at the Ritz Carlton for afternoon tea. It was a freezing cold, December day with the threat of snow hanging over the city. My Father's driver dropped me off in front of the Ritz and told me to call him when I was ready to leave. I was wrapped up tightly in my black, winter coat and although the door was only a few steps away, the cold air cut through me like a knife. The doorman greeted me as I rushed passed him into the warmth of the building.

Kirstin was already sitting at a small table in the middle of the tea room, waiting for me. She gave me a little wave, a slight wiggle of her fingers, while the seating host took my coat and hung it up for me. I was wearing a long-sleeved, black tunic dress that stopped above my knees over a pair of tight black leggings. My black leather boots came up to my knees, and my hair was up with a few stray pieces hanging like a frame around my face. As dressed up as I was, I was still nothing compared to Kirstin. Her outfit was almost identical to mine and yet she outdid me. It was no use competing with Kirstin when it came to fashion.

"Am I late?" I asked as I joined her at the table.

"No, no, I was just a little bit early," she replied.

"The traffic in the city was terrible today. It took me forever to get here."

"Oh, I knew it would be awful, that's why I left earlier than usual," she said with a hint of sarcasm as though I should have known better. *Insult number one*; she was starting early.

Our relationship had always been an interesting one. We kept each other close, but were more like rivals, than real friends. She was prettier and had better fashion sense. I, on the other hand, was smarter and much richer, and never for a second did I let her forget which of the two of us had the more important father. Kirstin had two older siblings, but my brother and I had a much closer relationship than she did with hers. I was also the one with the boyfriend. Brian was rich, hot, and mine; and Kirstin was insanely jealous.

We chatted politely over our tea, as politely as the two of us could at least. My tea was delicious as always and warmed up my insides against the cold weather. Kirstin was rambling on and on about her latest shopping escapade with her sister, but I was barely listening. I really didn't care and I was trying to figure out why I bothered to venture out on such a cold day only to listen to her nonsense, when she finally changed the subject.

"How is Craig?" She asked of my brother.

I put my tea cup down and said, "He's doing fine. He's been working with Father at the company during his winter break."

"Your Father is preparing him to take over his job one day, isn't he?"

"It would seem so. I'm just glad Craig decided to stay at home while he attends the University. I don't know what I'd do if I was all alone in that house with only my father for company. I think I would go crazy."

"From what I remember, Craig didn't exactly decide to stay at home on his own, did he?" She raised her eyebrow and smiled as she sipped her tea. *Insult number two;* she was on a roll.

She was referring to the time when Craig was applying to Universities and I begged him not to leave me. And when I say begged I mean it. I practically got on my hands and knees asking him to stay at home, at least until I graduated high school. One year later I was out of school, avoiding University at all costs, and Craig still lived at home. Craig and I had the best kind of sibling relationship. Sure, we argued from time to time, but we were close because we knew we were all each other had. Our father rarely spent time with us and as long as we kept ourselves out of serious trouble, he didn't care what we did.

"You and your brother have always been so close," Kirstin said mirroring my own thoughts.

"Yes, we have."

"My brother and I get along well enough, but we avoid each other most of the time. I mean it's a little strange to be *so* close to a brother, at least that's what I think," she sighed. "Oh well, what I think doesn't matter."

You've got that right, I thought.

"It's a shame though," she continued.

"What is?"

"That your mother died before she could give you a sister. You don't know how much you're missing not having another girl in the house to go shopping with and to talk to." *Insult number three.*

What was that American saying? Three strikes and you're out? Well Kirstin would have been out if Craig and Brian hadn't shown up at that exact moment. I swear Craig and I had some sort of telepathic connection because his timing was always perfect.

"Brian came by looking for you," Craig said when he reached our table, "and we decided to join you two girls."

"You're timing is perfect, as always," I gave Craig my one-more-second-and-I-would-have-killed-her look which he understood immediately, stifling a chuckle.

Brian leaned down to give me a kiss on the check. "Are you girls finished?" he asked.

"Not really..." Kirstin started.

"Absolutely," I finished.

"I was thinking we could go for a walk," he suggested.

"A walk? In this weather, are you crazy?" Kirstin was appalled by the idea.

Honestly, going for a walk sounded like the worst idea I'd ever heard, but in an effort to not sound like Kirstin, I said, "Sure, I could use some fresh air."

There was a small park near the hotel that was ideal for our walk. Brian helped me back into my coat and took my hand as we stepped out onto the street. Craig was being polite, listening to Kirstin's incessant chatter about nothing in particular, regularly responding with a "yes" or a "no" whenever necessary. When I looked behind me, he caught my eye and gave me his please-rescue-me look. We were halfway through the park when the first snowflakes started to fall.

"I think that's my cue to go back," Kirstin said.

"It's only snow," I replied. I loved the snow.

"I don't want to get all wet. Craig you wouldn't mind taking me back, would you? There's no reason why Brian and Mari can't continue their walk."

"Um…" Craig didn't know how to respond.

"It's okay, Craig." I said. "Brian and I will finish our walk around the park and then head back. Could you call our driver and tell him I'll be ready to leave soon?"

"Alright, I can do that. See you in a bit then?"

I nodded and they left. I could tell Craig felt uncomfortable leaving me, but I couldn't understand why. Brian *was* my boyfriend and Craig never felt strange about leaving us alone before. I had an uneasy feeling in the pit of my stomach and I wished I hadn't sent Craig away.

Brian and I walked a little further. The park looked so beautiful in the snow and when we reached the small, stone bridge at the center of the park, I stopped to look at the frozen pond below. I leaned over the edge of the bridge to look at the water, and I could feel Brian's eyes watching me.

"I have to tell you something," his face and tone were very serious.

"Is something wrong?" I asked.

He shook his head, "I asked Kirstin to steal Craig away so that we could be alone. I want to talk to you."

I laughed, "You could have said so. Craig would've gone willingly. What do you want to talk about?"

"I want to talk to you about the future. *Our* future. "

"Our future?" I wasn't sure I liked the sound of that.

Brian nodded, "I know we're both really young and not sure what we want yet, but there's one thing I *know* that I want."

"And what's that?"

"You," he paused. I turned away from him and looked at the water. I didn't know what to say. He continued: "Whenever I think about my future I see a big house and a job at the oil company, probably working for your brother, but more than any of that, I see you. I see you waiting for me at home every night. I see us together at events and making headlines. We would look so good together on the front pages of the newspapers. I even see our kids. Mari, I can't imagine my life without you. I want to marry you...soon."

"Are you proposing to me?" I was in shock.

"I think so," he thought for a minute. "Yes, I'm proposing to you. I know I'm not down on one knee, and I don't have a ring yet. We can do all that stuff later. I just wanted to tell you that this is the direction I'm heading in our relationship and I want you to start thinking about it too."

I was so confused. Marriage? Was he crazy? The first thought that came to my mind was Mother's journal. She said she wanted me to learn from her mistakes, but which ones was she talking about? Her whole life turned out to be a series of mistakes, one after the other, but where did they all begin? I knew the answer: they began with her marriage to my father.

"I talked to your father," Brian continued. "He agreed that a marriage between us would be beneficial to everyone and he gave me his blessing, so you don't need to worry about him."

"My father? You spoke to my father...and he said yes?" It was more than I could take. Sure, I always assumed I would get married one day, and I guess deep down I knew it would probably be Brian. His proposal came sooner than I thought it would and caught me completely off guard. My mother's words were bouncing around inside my head, intermingling with Brian's. She married too young and she married the wrong man, but which was the mistake? Which one applied to me? Was Brian the wrong man? Or was I too young?

"He says that if I continue to work hard at the company," Brian went on, "then he has no problem with us getting married sooner rather than later. Of course, only if you agree as well."

Brian paused, looking at me for an answer, but I still couldn't give him one. I kept trying to envision a future with him, and the scary thing was that I could. I could see every detail of what he described. I saw myself attending events in beautiful gowns and in cocktail dresses, with my arm draped through his, and everyone watching us. I saw myself as the stay at home wife who shopped and met her girlfriends for expensive lunches. I saw myself having children that looked like me and Brian mixed together and I saw Ruth holding our baby in a nursery. It was weird to see Ruth in my picture of the future. Would she raise my children the same way she raised me and Craig? Was I going to turn into one of those rich mothers who handed her children to the nanny whenever she was bored or didn't feel like changing a diaper? Was Joseph still going to be cooking my meals? My mother hired a nanny and a cook when she got sick because she needed help. My father kept the nanny and the cook because he didn't want to take care of us. I saw the future Brian described, and I hated every bit of it.

He was still talking when I interrupted him to say, "I think we should break up."

"Break up? What do you mean? I just proposed." It was his turn to feel confused.

40

"I don't want to marry you," I said. "I'm not even sure I want to get married at all. I don't want to make the same mistakes my mother did."

"I don't understand. What does this have to do with your mother?"

"My mother got married when she was a teenager and it killed her."

"Your mother died from pneumonia, not because she was married."

"Physically, yes she died from pneumonia, but figuratively, emotionally, marrying my father is what killed her."

"You're being dramatic," Brian said.

I shook my head, "No, I'm not. I found an old journal she wrote when she was sick. She wrote it for Craig and me to read because she wanted us to learn from her mistakes. She said she wished she never got married, that we were the only good things that came out of it. Our father tricked her into marrying him when she was too young, stole her away from her home, and then he killed her by ignoring her and lying to her. The fact that my father said yes to you makes me certain that saying no is the right decision."

"It wouldn't be like that for us," he pleaded. "We're not your parents, we could make this work and I promise I will never hurt you the way he hurt your mother."

I was beginning to get frustrated with the entire conversation, "Do you even hear yourself, Brian? You're proposing to me and not once have you said that you love me."

"What?"

"Do you love me, Brian?"

He was taken aback by the question. "I'm not sure how to answer you," he finally said.

"It's a simple yes or no question. Do you love me?"

"I can't win, no matter how I answer you. You're setting me up for a test I can't pass."

"What are you talking about? I want to know if you care about me. You're asking me to marry you, so you must love me, right?"

"If I say yes, you're going to say that I must be lying to you to get my way and if I say no then you're going to walk away from me. I can't win."

He did know me. He was right of course, no matter what answer he chose to give, I would have found an excuse to say no to his proposal. "I'll make this easy on you then. My answer is no and will *always* be no." I turned my back to him and walked away.

"Where is he?!" I shouted at Ruth as I walked into the house.

"Who? You mean your father?" She asked.

"Of course I mean Father," I snapped. "Where is he? Is he here?"

"I believe he's in his office."

I pushed by her and rushed down the hallway towards his office.

"He asked not to be disturbed," Ruth called after me, but I ignored her and barged straight into the room without knocking.

"How could you?!" I yelled at him. Father was sitting behind his desk, a pen in one hand and the phone receiver in the other.

"Excuse me, gentlemen," he said into the phone. "I have something personal to take care of. Let us reconvene in about ten minutes." Ten minutes was all the time he was willing to spend on his obviously upset daughter. "This must be important because you know better than to interrupt me when I'm working. What is it you wish to say to me?"

"How dare you go behind my back and agree to marry me off."

"Ah I see, Brian has asked you to marry him. I suppose you've refused him, correct?"

"Of course I've refused. I'm seventeen! I don't want to be married!"

Father nodded pensively, almost in agreement, "I understand your concern; I thought the very same thing myself. But after some thought and a conversation with Brian, I think it's a perfectly acceptable solution to your current position."

"My current position? What's that supposed to mean?"

He sighed, "Mari, it is time that you made some decisions about your future. Can you tell me what it is that you do all day? You are not in school and you've shown no interest in pursuing a career of any sort. You are useless to me if you continue down this path, and I will *not* stand for it! The way I see it, you have three options to choose from. You can apply to University for the upcoming spring semester, you can marry Brian, or you can join me at the company, working your way up from the bottom. If you choose any of these options then I will continue to indulge you in your current lifestyle, provided you pursue the option seriously and make progress. Otherwise, you will have to leave this house. I will withdraw all financial support and remove you from my life. I refuse to support you while you do nothing. Do you understand me?"

I was unable to speak. Tears were pooling in my eyes and my throat was beginning to close, but I would not cry in front of him. I wouldn't give him the satisfaction.

"I am aware that this is a big decision, so I will give you a few days to think about it."

"And which of the options," I found my words, "would you like me to choose?"

"The sooner you are married, Mari, the sooner you become someone else's burden to bear. If you'll excuse me, that will be all for now, I have more important matters to attend to."

I slowly turned away from him and took a step towards the office door.

"And Mari," he called after me, "Don't disappoint me. You will regret it if you do."

★◆★

I slammed my bedroom door shut and threw myself on my bed. The tears I felt earlier vanished and

I was left only with anger. I was so ashamed of myself. I went into his office to stand up for myself and to put Father in his place, but he reversed everything on me. I knew eventually he would put his foot down about University and make me go, but I never imagined he would force me to make such a big decision in such a short time. I should have known better. None of the options he gave me were ones that I could live with for the rest of my life and I knew I couldn't make it on my own. I was stuck and I desperately needed help.

Ruth entered my room without knocking and sat down beside me. She pushed some of the hair from my face and said, "Shh, child. Everything is gonna be alright."

"Don't you ever knock?" I lashed out at her even though I knew it wasn't her fault.

"You know better than to talk to me like that, girl," she warned.

"What am I supposed to do?"

"You're going to stay calm and think," she said as if it was the simplest thing in the world.

I stood up and began to pace around my bedroom, "Stay calm? That's your advice? Do you have any idea what Father just did to me?"

Ruth nodded, but remained quiet.

"You were listening behind the door, weren't you?" I stopped and looked at her.

"I was."

I wasn't surprised, "I had a feeling you were there. Well, you heard him, what do you think I should do?"

"Let's talk about it. What were the three choices he gave you?"

I resumed my pacing and listed the items, counting them off with my fingers, "One, I go to school. Two, I marry Brian. Three, I go to work for him."

"You are very young and I don't believe you love this boy, Brian. Marrying him would be a big mistake, so we eliminate option two."

"Working for my father is also out of the question. Did you hear what he said about it? He said I would have to start from the bottom and work my way up. Craig and Brian asked for jobs and he gave them training and high level positions, but because I am a girl I will have to work my way up from the bottom? I don't think so! Plus, working for him would make me crazy; we hate each other. So, option three is out too."

"That leaves you with the first option."

"Going to University," I paused and thought for a moment. "I can't do it."

"Why not? What's wrong with going back to school?"

"I'm not cut out for school. I never was. The thought of going back makes my stomach turn. Don't you remember all those years of helping me with hours of homework, just so I could earn mediocre grades? I'm too stupid for school."

"You are *not* stupid. Don't you dare say that."

"The only reason I got through school was because Father made generous donations to the schools and education system; the teachers were too afraid to fail me. And the only way I'll get into a University is because of his name."

"So then, what do you do?"

"I don't know!" I started pacing again. "Why did Mother have to be the one that died? If Father had died instead I wouldn't even have to think about this. I could have been an entirely different person. I could have been happy!"

"There is no sense dwelling on things you cannot change. It won't help you."

"I know. I just wish I knew what Mother would say right now. You were close to her, what would she tell me to do?"

"You're right," Ruth replied. "I was close to your mother, but I can't say how she would answer you. I do know that she wanted you to be happy, no matter what, and she knew your father would never provide such happiness for you and Craig. These options he gave you will never make you happy; you must come up with a better option for yourself. What *will* make you happy, Mari?"

"The only other choice I have is to leave home and I'm not capable of doing that. I'll never make it on my own. Where would I go? What would I do? How would I live? I am entirely dependent on my father and he knows it. I'm not brave enough to leave everything and try to make it on my own." I slumped down next to Ruth.

52

"Think about it for a minute, child. What is it that you want from this life?"

"I want my mother. I want to know who she was. I feel like I'll never be able to move on until I know why she ended up here."

"Perhaps you already know her better than you think."

Ruth pushed something towards me, then stood and left my room. I looked down beside me on the bed and saw my mother's journal. Maybe I did know more about her than I thought. I flipped through the pages and by the time I reached the end, I made a decision.

Chapter 4

I'll never forget how nervous I felt sitting in London's Heathrow Airport waiting for my flight to depart. I kept thinking that at any second my father would plop down in the seat beside me and say, "Alright young lady, enough of this foolishness," and drag me back home. The longer I sat in the airport the faster my heart beat. I envisioned my father's face on the face of every man in Heathrow. He checked my suitcase at the front desk. He was eating pizza at one of the restaurants and he was running to catch a connecting flight. There he was buying duty-free in the shop across from my gate. He was reading a newspaper and he smiled at me as I boarded the plane. He was everywhere, and yet nowhere.

The plane took forever to take off, but once the wheels left the runway and England started to shrink beneath us, my nervousness turned to excitement. I did it! I wanted to leap for joy. I had escaped! If anyone at home noticed me missing it was too late for them to stop me. I had no idea what was awaiting me in Nigeria, but that's the whole point of an adventure isn't it? I fell asleep during the flight and by the time I woke up the pilot was announcing our arrival at Port Harcourt International Airport. I opened the shutter on my window and caught my first glimpse of what was to become my new home: Nigeria.

There wasn't much to see from the runway. Bright green grass lined the edges of the landing strip and spread out over the land, stopping when it reached a line of trees in the distance. Inside, the airport was packed with travelers coming or going from everywhere. I pushed and shoved my way through the crowd to the baggage claim and was relieved to see my suitcase had arrived with me. Once I retrieved my bag I rolled it behind me over to the customs line.

Going through customs in Nigeria was no joke. Soldiers in camouflage uniforms, holding very big guns, blocked the doors that led into the country—definitely not men I wanted to mess with. Custom agents sat behind bullet-proof windows and asked each person a series of questions. What is the purpose of your visit? How long do you intend to stay in the country? Occasionally a person was asked to step aside and follow one of the soldiers through a different set of doors. Those doors meant trouble, big trouble.

Nervously, I slid my passport through the opening in the window. The customs agent, a man who spent his life sizing people up and deciding their fate in a matter of seconds, began his inspection of me. He carefully examined the passport, comparing the picture with my face, and studied me with his judgmental eyes. Finally, satisfied that my passport was authentic, he asked his questions.

"What is the purpose of your visit?"

"I'm on an extended holiday," I answered.

"How long do you intend to stay in the country?"

"Several weeks."

The agent furrowed his brow at my answer. In truth, I didn't actually know how long I intended to stay; I hadn't planned that far ahead. He glared at me for a few seconds more, decided I wasn't a threat, and stamped my passport with the Nigerian seal.

"Thank you," I said as he slid the passport back to me. He grunted in reply and motioned me through the gates. I gave my suitcase a tug to get it rolling and took my first steps onto Nigerian soil.

Heat and humidity were the first things I noticed as I stood in front of the airport under the old, faded green lettering, "Port Harcourt International Airport." It was early December and hotter than anything I'd ever felt before. Only one day earlier I was standing in the snow in London. Most of the clothing I packed was for cold weather. One of the first things I was going to have to do was go shopping, which to me was not a bad way to start a holiday. I had two choices outside of the airport. I could hire a car to take me into Port Harcourt or I could take a bus to anywhere else in Nigeria. Port Harcourt was a city my mother mentioned in her journal, as one of the closest to the village where she grew up. My trip was all about walking in her footsteps and experiencing life the way she did. I hired a car, kind of like a taxi but more like a shuttle bus, and had the driver take me to a hotel in the city. There were several decent hotels, of which I chose the cheapest. I used cash to purchase a room for two weeks, knowing I would have to make a decision by then about my future in Nigeria. I left all but one of my credit cards at home, so that Father wouldn't be able to find me by tracking their use, which meant my money was going to run out by the end of two weeks, according to my rough calculations.

I went shopping, and bought clothing more appropriate for the hot weather—shorts, sandals, tanks, and tee-shirts—exploring and learning my way around the city as I did. I also bought a map from one of the shops and searched for Ogoniland on it, but it wasn't there. I learned later that the name Ogoniland was more like a nickname for the area rather than a town or village name. I asked around for several days and some people were able to point me in the right direction, but most didn't want to be bothered with my questions. It was at the end of my two weeks, when the cash was nearly gone and the hotel manager was eyeing my room, that I at last made a breakthrough.

I decided to venture into the Borikiri market, as recommended by the front desk at my hotel. I was told the market was a must-see and that there would be many people who might be able to help me. Borikiri market stretched for miles along the banks of the Bonny River. Colorful umbrellas marked each new stall of products, and thick, black smoke rose above the city from the fires blazing at the far end of the market. Hundreds of people were gathered to shop, buy, and bargain for all the different kinds of goods, mostly food, that were being sold. The market was overwhelming and I stuck out like a sore thumb amongst the crowds of people. I also had the strange feeling that I was being watched. My last bit of money and my passport were hidden in an inner pocket in a pair of shorts I bought in the city. The hotel staff warned me of pick pockets on my arrival and told me to make sure I kept a close eye on my belongings and on the people around me. Being in the big market crowd I understood exactly what they meant. People were everywhere on all sides of me, bumping into and shoving me aside. There were strangers' hands on me constantly, and I fought down my growing sense of panic and claustrophobia. I absolutely hate crowds.

The further I walked in the market, the thicker the smoke became. Every breath I took burned the back of my throat and made my eyes water. I stopped at one of the market stalls and bought a beautiful, handmade scarf. I wrapped it around my head and face, mimicking the other women I saw in the market, to block the smell of smoke. Toward the far end of the market I could see the flames of large fires burning and an assembly of people gathering around them. Curiosity drove me in the direction of the fires. Piles of old car tires were set aflame and were the cause of the awful smell and black smoke that rose over the market as I pressed forward through the crowd; I wanted to see what everyone was watching. In between the fires were men in groups of three, each with a male cow, or steer, between them. The eyes of the animal closest to me were wild and panicked, in fear of what was to come. I watched as two of the men pushed the steer to the ground and climbed onto its back to hold it steady. The beast screamed and thrashed, but stood no chance against the men. I watched as the third man took an old, rusty machete and used it to slit the beast's throat. All six steer were treated the same. The blood drained from the animals into a make-shift trough dug into the ground leading it past the crowd and down to the river bank. Six steer's worth of blood rushed by my feet staining the ground and the water red.

My stomach was turning inside me. I pushed back through the people, back the way I'd come, and found a clear stretch of the shore, where I threw my breakfast up into the river. People stopped to stare at me before moving on to purchase hunks of beef from the newly slaughtered steer. The smell of meat cooking began to mix with the already strong smell of burning rubber as the butchers placed the meat over the open flames to dry.

I forced myself to straighten up using a corner of my new scarf to wipe my mouth. I stood staring into one of the tire fires, my stomach empty and my throat sore. I wanted to leave, to turn around and never think about those fires again, but there was something about them that drew me in. Seeing an animal killed and then chopped into sections was disgusting to me, but the longer I thought about it the more I understood. Although I came from a place where butchering food in the streets was completely unheard of, I understood that it was a necessary evil in life. They weren't killing animals, they were feeding people. I was going to have to grow a stronger stomach if I was going to live in Nigeria.

Someone was watching me from the opposite side of the fire as I was lost in thought. I could sense his eyes long before I saw him. He was a young man, not much older than me, white, with light brown hair and the brightest, green eyes I'd ever seen. He was attractive and made me feel uneasy under his gaze. I was uncomfortably aware of how terrible I looked; dirty, sweaty, and probably pale from throwing up. My cheeks flushed red at the thought of him having witnessed my case of a weak stomach. I broke away from his stare by turning my back to him. I could still feel his eyes boring into my back as I walked away.

I wanted to go back to my hotel room, to wash the grime from my body and to have an ice cold drink to soothe my burning throat, but the hotel was a long way off. I was on the furthest end of the market. I moved slowly, no longer fighting the crowd, but rather flowing with it. The further away from the smell of meat and rubber, the better I began to feel.

"Hey, watch it!"

"Look out!"

"You, stop there!"

I was more than halfway through the market, back to where the vendors were selling fruits and vegetables when the commotion began. A young boy, no more than fourteen, with fair skin that was filthy, was running through the people, pushing past anyone in his way. I quickly stepped sideways and he barely missed me as he ran by. He ran, weaved, and bobbed his way around the market stalls with government soldiers chasing after him. The soldiers were angry and I found myself rooting for the boy to get away. He didn't. The soldiers trapped him between two stalls of fruit and then escorted him away from the crowd. They brought him to the edge of the road next to a parked jeep, where a man in an officer's uniform was waiting. The boy hid his fear well, but he knew he was in trouble.

"You again?" The officer asked. His uniform was different from the others, marking him as a man-in-charge. Everyone called him Captain.

"Hey Captain," the boy replied. "You mind tellin' your henchmen here to let me go?" In response the two soldiers holding him by the arms, tightened their grip. "I'll take that as a no."

"Well, well, Zack. Caught again? What did I say would happen the next time I caught you stealing?" The captain asked.

"Stealing? Is that what you think I did? I didn't steal nothin' Captain, honest."

"Is that so?" The Captain proceeded to check the boy's pockets and clothing. Several pieces of fruit, and various other small items, tumbled out of the boy's pockets. "What do you call all of this?"

"I bought all of that."

"Can you prove it?" The boy didn't answer; he knew it was time to keep his mouth shut. "I told you last time that you would be punished. No more chances. Put him in the jeep and take him to the prison," he commanded his soldiers. "I'm going to make an example of you. Ogoni scum," he spit on the ground in front of the boy.

Ogoni scum? Had I heard him right? Was the boy from one of the Ogoni villages? I had to find out.

"Wait!" I shouted at the soldiers. "Wait!" The boy was already sitting in the back seat of the jeep with his hands cuffed behind his back. The Captain eyed me curiously as I approached. "Zack," I said remembering his name from their conversation. "I've been looking for you everywhere. Where have you been? Did you get everything I sent you for?" I completely ignored the soldiers and the Captain and focused all my attention on the boy, willing him to play along with me. He didn't even miss a beat.

"Yeah, I got all the stuff, but these guys here think I stole it," he replied.

"You know this boy?" The Captain interrupted, stepping forward.

"Yes sir, he's a friend of mine. I'm so sorry, this is entirely my fault. We were separated in the crowd." I was playing the *I'm-a-bimbo-but-I'm-harmless-so-let-me-go* trick on him, or what I liked to call a Kirstin, and I saw that it was working. I just needed to put the cherry on top, "I'm so sorry again, please let me give you something for your trouble," I took the last of my cash out of my inner pocket and placed it in the Captain's hand.

The Captain looked from the money in his hand, to me, and then to Zack in the jeep. After a few anxious seconds, he nodded to his men and they dragged Zack back out of the jeep. I was flooded with relief and, I must admit, was pretty proud of myself.

"You were lucky this time, boy," the Captain said before we walked away. "Next time I catch you, will be the last."

"Thank you sir," I replied. "I can assure you, you won't be having any more trouble from either of us."

The Captain and his men got into their jeep and took off. Zack and I walked a good distance away before we spoke. Zack was blonde with pale green eyes and skin that was tanned from living in the sun. There was something very familiar about his looks, almost as if I had met him somewhere before. He was thin and scrappy and liked to act tough.

"So, who are you anyway?" He asked me.

"How about a 'thank you' since I just saved your butt," I replied.

"That *was* kinda cool, what you did back there, but no favors come without a price here. So, what do you want?"

"Okay, you're right. I have a question for you."

"Go ahead, ask it," to emphasize his "toughness" he crossed his arms over his chest and spat on the ground.

"I heard that Captain call you an 'Ogoni scum.' Are you from Ogoniland?"

"So what if I am?"

"It's just that I've come all the way here from London to visit someone in Ogoniland and I don't know how to get there. I was wondering if you could maybe give me directions or something."

"I guess..."

"Zack!" A man's voice shouted. Zack looked nervous. Another young man with similar features was crossing through the market crowd making his way toward us. I recognized him immediately as the young man who stared at me over the fires on the butcher's side of the market. I began to feel nervous too.

"Zack where have you been?!" The young man was angry. "I heard someone was being arrested for stealing, it better not have been you!"

"Do I look like I'm being arrested?"

"Don't get smart with me."

"Everything's fine," I interrupted.

The young man furrowed his brow as he recognized me, "Who are you?"

"My name is Mari. I was just asking Zack for directions to the Ogoni villages; maybe you can help me?"

He copied Zack's defiant stance and asked, "Why do you want to go to the villages?"

"It's personal." We stood eyeing one another, neither of us making a move to offer more information. He studied me curiously and I stood my ground.

Reaching a decision the young man nodded curtly and said, "We leave for our village in an hour. Meet us at the meat market; we'll give you a ride."

"Thank you! That's great, I just need to get my stuff and check out of my hotel."

"We drive an old, white, pick-up truck. You'll know it when you see it, you can't miss it. One hour, we won't wait a minute more, got it?"

"Got it."

"All right then. Oh, and try not to hurl when you pass by the meat this time."

I blushed in shame. *So he did see me throwing up* I thought. He walked away and Zack followed flashing me a mischievous grin. One hour. In one hour I would be one step closer to finding my mother's family.

I rushed to the hotel, packed my suitcase, checked out, and ran back through the market as quickly as I could. I didn't want to keep Zack and the young man, whoever he was, waiting for me, or more likely leaving without me; they were the only lead I had. My suitcase was heavy, filled with clothes from London and all the purchases I made in Port Harcourt. The small wheels kept getting stuck in holes and on rocks. I hurried by the recently cooked meat, careful not to look too closely. The ground around the fires and even the air itself was black from the burning tires. The white, pick-up truck was easy to spot against the black landscape. Zack and the young man were standing at the back of the truck putting in the last of the supplies they bought from the market.

"Right on time," the young man said. "Let's go," he shut the gate on the truck and walked around to the driver's side. I stayed where I was. My suitcase was too heavy for me to lift over the side of the truck and although I didn't want to ask, I needed help.

"Do you mind?" I asked him. He rolled his eyes and walked back over to help me. He lifted my suitcase as though it weighed nothing and threw it into the back of the truck.

"Hey, careful with that!" Everything I owned was in that suitcase. I peeked into the truck bed to see where it landed—big mistake. There was half of a cow carcass packed into the back of the truck, my suitcase lying right beside it. I relived the slaughter of the steer and nearly lost the contents of my stomach again. "Why do you have half of a dead cow in your truck?" I asked.

"Because a whole one wouldn't fit." He and Zack exchanged a high five and a fitful of laughter over his comeback. I was disgusted. I gave him a dirty look as I watched him get into the driver's seat.

Zack stood by the passenger door motioning me to get in before him. I shook my head, "I'm not sitting in the middle seat." I had two reasons; one was because I knew the ride was going to be bumpier in the middle and I didn't want to end up sick again and two; I wanted to be as far away from the young man as possible. Sitting next to him for who knew how long, while riding on bumpy dirt roads, in such a small amount of space, was not my idea of fun.

"I hate the middle seat," Zack argued.

74

"Will you two get in already? Hurry up," the young man was annoyed.

"You're the youngest, you should sit in the middle," I said to Zack.

"Hey girl, either get in the middle seat or get in the back with the meat," the young man ordered.

I felt my face blanch. I was outnumbered and definitely not getting into the back with the meat. With little choice, I crawled into the middle seat, crammed between two complete strangers, on my way to a place that I didn't know and that wasn't even on the map. Zack, satisfied with himself, sat comfortably beside me staring out of his open window. I was right about the bumpy roads. I constantly had to put my hand on the dashboard to steady myself. I tried so hard to keep my body from touching either of the boys, but it was no use in such a small truck. I gave up after a while and relaxed my muscles. My leg grazed the edge of the young man's and I saw him flinch out of the corner of my eye. *Well, if he doesn't like it, it's his own fault. He should have made Zack sit in the middle.*

We drove in silence, not a word between us, for quite some time. I stared out the front window watching the landscape change as we drove further away from the city. Several times we could see large clouds of black smoke reaching up into the sky in the distance. Sometimes we were even close enough to see the orange flames below the smoke. The flames were being shot out of pipelines leading away from large industrial plants.

"What are they doing there?" I asked.

"Gas flaring," the young man answered. "When the oil companies bring the oil up from the ground they also bring up all kinds of gases. They take whatever they can use or sell later, but they burn off the rest."

"What kind of gas do they burn?" I don't know what kind of answer I was expecting or if the young man would even have an answer, but I was curious. I lived off the oil money my whole life but I never knew how the oil companies worked.

"Usually methane or sulfur compounds."

"You're telling me that every flaming pipe we've passed is burning off sulfur and methane? Those are like two of the most dangerous gases to breathe in," I said remembering my lessons from Science class. "They're releasing that stuff into the air right around the corner from where people live!"

"Welcome to the Niger River Delta, home of the oil rivers." He gestured out the front window with his hand; there were more gas flares in the distance.

He grew quiet again and, in an effort to keep the conversation going, I said, "I never asked you your name."

"Danny," he answered. *Danny*. The name suited him. He was older than me, but not by much; early twenties was my guess. He and Zack shared the same eyes and hair color, but Danny's were a shade darker. His hair was more brown than blonde, with highlights from the sun, and his green eyes were electric.

"Thank you for doing this," I said. They were saving me a lot of time and money taking me to the village.

"Apparently I'm the one who should be thanking you," Danny said. "Zack told me what you did for him in the market."

"Oh, that was nothing, I'm glad I was able to help. I'm also glad I bumped into the two of you. Are you related?"

"We're brothers."

"I thought so, you look a lot alike."

"What did you say your name was again?" I knew he'd forgotten my name.

"Mari," I replied.

"That's an unusual name, is it short for something?"

"Marienela."

He whistled, "That's a mouthful, no wonder you go by Mari. What's it mean?"

"I don't know," I muttered. My name was always a talking point. People would ask: what does it mean? Where did it come from? Why did your parents pick it? My mother chose the name because she liked its meaning,—at least that's what Ruth told me—but she never told anyone what it meant. The secret died with her. She didn't even mention it in the journal she wrote to me and Craig. Father hated the name, but like me, he was stuck with it. My name was a soft spot for the both of us, a topic we never discussed, especially with strangers.

"You don't know what your name means?" Danny asked.

"Who says it means anything at all?"

"Long names like that usually have a special meaning."

"Well, mine doesn't," and my tone closed the subject.

A few minutes later, Danny picked up the conversation with a new line of questioning. "Why do you want to go to the Ogoni villages?"

"I'm visiting someone," I said.

"Who?"

"An old friend."

"Really?" He seemed skeptical. "Who are you friends with in my village?"

"I'm not even sure they live in *your* village."

"What's their name?"

I gave in, "Naomi. I'm here to see a woman named Naomi and her son, Jim."

"You know Naomi and Jim?" Zack perked up.

"Sort of."

"How do you know them?" Both boys asked at once.

"None of this has anything to do with you," I said. "Look, if you're worried I'm up to some sort of trouble, I promise you, I'm not. I'm just here on holiday, visiting a couple of old friends."

"See, that's the part that's bugging me," Danny said. "I've lived in the village my whole life and I've never seen you visit before. Naomi and Jim haven't gone on any holidays either. How can you be old friends if you've never met them before?"

"They knew my mother," I said under my breath.

"Who's your mother?"

"Her name was Lila," my voice just above a whisper. Upon hearing my mother's name Danny clamped his mouth shut. He was either satisfied with my answers or...he recognized her name.

His silence didn't last long enough. "How long are you going to stay?"

I reached my breaking point. I was tired, hot, angry, and anxious. I'd had enough. "As long as I bloody want to!" I shouted at him. "I've told you enough, none of it is your business. I helped your brother in exchange for a ride and that's that. I'm not going to be interrogated by some country boy who knows nothing about me..."

"I know plenty about you, believe me," he cut me off. "The way you're dressed, the size of your suitcase, your pale skin, soft hands, and bourgeois attitude all tell me that you come from money. Big money. You come from some stuck-up, wealthy,

English family and you either ran away or are on some sort of punishment. I'm betting you're a runaway. So what happened? Daddy didn't buy you a pony, so you ran away to some country your Mommy used to talk about?"

"How dare you!"

"That must be it. Let me ask you: how many ponies do you have?"

"You are such a..."

"Stop it!" Zack yelled over the both of us. "Can you two stop it, we're almost there."

Zack's interruption put an end to the argument. Our drive lasted only a few minutes more, a few more minutes of awkwardness, and we were there. The truck climbed the slope of a steep hill, Danny pressing hard against the gas pedal. At the top of the hill, we were overlooking the village. The village was nestled below, between the bank of a river and the edge of a barren section of land once used for farming. In the background, not too far away, I could see the edge of the Nigerian jungle, the strange trees reaching out like arms. There were multitudes of little hut-like homes crowded together, one practically on top of the other, lining the banks of the river and spreading out towards the field. The river water was dark, the edges of the shore black. Off in the distance, the backdrop of it all, a large plume of smoke rose into the sky like an omen above the village.

Danny drove us into the center of the village, an empty space in the center of all the homes, bustling with people. The center was flat, dusty ground and in the middle there was a line of people waiting behind some sort of pump. We drove by too quickly for me to see what the pump was for, but whatever it was the people wanted or needed it. The line was one of the longest I'd ever seen. Many small roads and paths led to and from the village center making it accessible for everyone. Danny parked the truck near one of the paths.

"Naomi and Jim live at the end of this road," he said. "They're the last on the right closest to the river. You'll know when you get there."

"You're not going to drive me there?" In answer, Danny got out of the truck and unloaded my suitcase from the back. I started to panic on the inside; I really didn't want to be left alone even if my only option was being stuck with him.

Danny shook his head, "I have more important errands to run. You can walk the rest of the way." He waited for me to climb out of the truck. He got back into the driver's seat and slammed the door shut. I was standing outside of his open window with my suitcase next to me.

"How am I supposed to get my suitcase all the way down this road?"

"It has wheels, doesn't it?" He restarted the engine.

I approached his window, "Okay look, I'm sorry about our little argument, we both had our reasons, but please don't leave me here like this. I don't know where I am or how to find Naomi. Please just take me to her home."

"Can't, sorry. Don't worry, you'll be fine."

He left me standing there at the end of Naomi's road, suitcase in hand, leaving a giant dust cloud in his wake.

Dragging my suitcase on the bumpy path turned out to be the challenge I knew it would be. The bag would not cooperate with me and every time it felt like it was back on track I would roll over a rock and the bag would either get stuck or fall completely over. My arm was tired and I was tempted to ditch the bag altogether. On top of all that, I had no idea where I was going. There were a lot of people walking on the path, coming out from their homes or from other paths between the homes. I picked an older woman, who didn't seem as busy as all the others, and approached her to ask for directions.

"Excuse me," her back was turned to me. When I got her attention she took one look at me and jerked back. She slowly backed away from me and made the sign of the cross over herself. "I'm sorry I scared you. I'm looking for Naomi and her son Jim; do you know where they live?"

The woman raised her arm and pointed towards the end of the path. I saw that the path widened as it went along and the homes became more and more sparse. The woman was still eyeing me suspiciously.

"Thank you," I said. I walked away from her, but I peeked over my shoulder to see if she was still watching me. She stepped out onto the path and began to follow me keeping several paces behind. I acted as normally as I could as I continued walking. I frequently checked to see if she was still following me. Not only was she still there, but others had joined her. Older people and some very young children trailed behind me on my way to Naomi. I started to get nervous. There were so many people; if they wanted to rob me or murder me, I wouldn't stand a chance. My safest bet was to find Naomi quickly, and hope that she could help me. My suitcase hit another rock that flipped it over and onto the ground.

"Great," I muttered. I bent over to pick it up and got a better glimpse of the crowd watching me. They were all stopped, the older woman in the lead, watching every move I made. Her eyes never left me.

"Naomi?" I asked again. She used her head, thrusting her chin up, to point at the very last home, closest to the river, exactly as Danny had said. I took a careful step backwards in that direction and then I turned and moved swiftly to the hut. There was no door, only a piece of cloth hanging in the entryway.

"Hello?" I called out. "Is anybody there?"

There were shuffling noises coming from inside. Behind me there were whispers coming from my audience. The noise inside grew louder and the door curtain fluttered. A hand reached out and gently lifted the curtain away.

A woman stepped outside, saw me, and gasped.

Chapter 5

A clay pot slipped from the woman's hands and shattered on the ground.

"Are you Naomi?" I asked the shocked woman.

"Mari?" She squinted at me, "Is that really you?"

"Yes," I breathed out in relief.

"Oh my...what on earth are you doing here, child?" Her arms reached out to me, first touching my face and then pulling me to her. She squeezed me tightly and I held her back. I'm not sure what kind of welcome I was expecting, but I wasn't disappointed. "Let me get a good look at you." She released me from her grip and made me spin in a slow circle in front of her. "You are the exact image of your mother."

While I was twirling I realized the crowd was still standing on the road watching me. "Um, Naomi, maybe you could tell these people who I am. They're starting to scare me a bit."

Naomi stepped past me and addressed my audience with a smile and her hands up in surrender, "It's alright," she told them. "This is Lila's daughter, not her ghost. Her name is Marienela."

A wave of relief spread over the people. Some applauded, some smiled, a few of the children waved to me and I waved back. Everyone left then, their curiosity satisfied. Naomi grabbed my hand as the last of them were leaving and pulled me inside her hut. He hut was small, only one rounded room, with a dirt floor, two small mattresses, and all of the supplies and clothing stored in big wooden boxes, like chests. Naomi pushed two of the boxes away from the wall into the middle of the room and motioned for me to sit on one.

"They're not super comfortable," she told me, "but we make do."

It felt so good to let go of my suitcase and sit down. "Thank you," I said.

"I cannot believe that you're here! You must tell me everything."

"I hardly know where to begin," I replied.

"Tell me why you've come."

I started from when I found Mother's journal and told her everything. I told her about Ruth, and Joseph and Craig, and about our life in London. I told her about Brian's ridiculous proposal and of Father's ultimatum. I left no detail out as I described my reasons for leaving, and she listened intently to every word, even nodding in approval when I spoke of Ruth's advice to me.

"I like this Ruth," she said.

I continued, telling her about the flight and my two weeks in Port Harcourt. She laughed when I told her I threw up in the meat market and shook her head when I told her about Zack getting into trouble. I even mentioned my argument with Danny and complained about him dropping me off and leaving me on my own. She didn't like that part either, but chose to defend him by saying:

"He knew you would be safe here."

"But I wasn't," I protested. "All those people were following me; any one of them could've robbed or killed me."

Naomi shook her head, "They're old and some are superstitious, but they are all completely harmless.

They thought you were the ghost of your mother. I admit you gave me quite a shock as well."

"How *did* you know it was me?"

"I am not superstitious, I knew you were no ghost," she chuckled. "Your mother used to send me pictures of you and your brother. Even when you were very young you looked like her."

"Can you tell me about her?"

"Of course, child. I'll tell you everything you want to know."

"Would it be okay if I stayed here for a while? I'll keep out of your way and help you with some of your work. You could give me chores or..."

She raised her hand, "Nonsense. You are the daughter of my best and oldest friend, and you are welcome to stay with me and my son for as long as you wish. There is no need for you to work, but you can help if you want."

"I don't know how to thank you."

"You can keep me company and tell me all about your life in London. That is all I will ever ask of you."

I began to thank her again when a man entered the hut. He was tall and muscular, in his mid-twenties with short, black hair, dark skin, and almond eyes. He shared Naomi's features and didn't seem surprised to see me.

"Mari, this is my son Jim," Naomi introduced us. "Jim, this is Lila's daughter. She's come for a visit and is going to stay with us for a while."

Jim offered me his hand I shook it. "Everyone in the village is talking about you, you've made quite the impression already. It's nice to finally meet you."

"It's nice to meet you too," I blushed and he released my hand. "I hope my being here won't be an inconvenience for you."

"We always manage to find a way to squeeze in," he laughed. "We do it all the time in the village. People sleep wherever they fit, even if that means in their neighbor's bed. We are all a family here."

I immediately decided that I liked him. Jim was such a happy and positive person. In some ways he reminded me of Craig, whom I already missed. My arrival on their doorstep had to be an inconvenience, but neither of them ever showed it. They welcomed me into their home and their lives with open arms.

Jim made a new bed for me to sleep on and set it up inside their home. The three of us would have some difficulty squeezing into the small space, but somehow they found a way to make room for me. Naomi boiled water in a small pot so I could wash up and went back outside to give me privacy. I was grateful for the hot water and used it to wash away all of the grime my body collected in the market. I scrubbed my skin with a small cloth until it turned pink, then quickly donned new clothes and shoved my belongings beside the boxes so they would be out of the way.

Outside I heard the wheels of a car crunching up the dirt path and stopping in front of the hut. Jim offered a greeting to someone and I poked my head through the curtain doorway to see who arrived. The same white, pick-up truck that brought me to the village was parked in front of the hut, with Danny leaning against it. I pulled my head back inside quickly and pressed my body against the cool, mud wall. The last thing I wanted was to see him. I listened to their conversation and a realization made my heart sink into the pit of my stomach. Of course! I should have known the two of them would be friends; they grew up together in the same village.

"Thanks for letting me borrow the truck," Danny said to Jim. "Sorry it was so last minute, you know how these things go."

"You're welcome to it anytime, you know that," Jim answered. "How was the delivery?"

"Right on time."

"You're playing a dangerous game, Danny."

"Aren't we all?"

Naomi's voice came next, "Did you meet anyone interesting at the market today?"

"Is that your way of asking me about the girl? Did she get here okay?"

"She was a bit shaken up, but perfectly fine," Naomi replied. "Was it really necessary for you to leave her like that?"

"You have no idea how necessary it was."

"Now I know you know better than to act that way. I don't care what she said to you, there was no reason for such bad manners. Don't you let me hear about you doing anything like that again."

"Yes ma'am."

I smiled as Naomi gave him a well-deserved tongue lashing. He completely deserved it.

She finished by telling him, "You will apologize to her, immediately."

"Maybe some other time, I really need to get back home now." His voice seemed further away as though he was backing away from them. Naomi didn't say anything more to him. I heard Jim chuckle at his mother and I dared another glance outside. Danny was gone. Naomi turned her death stare, a look I later learned to avoid at all costs, onto me when I joined her by the small fire outside the hut.

"I'm sure you weren't completely blameless in your argument."

"He started it." That was the first and *only* time I ever answered back when Naomi was giving me her evil eye. I gulped and mimicked Danny's answer, "I mean, yes ma'am."

She nodded satisfied, and continued to cook dinner over the flames for the three of us. Dinner was a light, delicious chicken broth, the best I'd ever had in my life. We sat on logs around the fire, eating and telling stories. I barely noticed, but as we talked the sky grew dark and the stars began to rise. There were millions shining brightly in the sky above us, more than I'd ever seen beneath the lights of London.

"I've never seen so many!" I said aloud. Even during my two weeks in Port Harcourt, I never took the time to notice the difference in the sky. Jim and Naomi smiled in response and let me enjoy the view before declaring it to be bed time. Exhausted from all the excitement, I followed them into the hut without argument. I curled up on my new mattress—a large sewn sheet stuffed with hay—and instantly fell asleep.

I slept for a good portion of the next day and awoke stiff from sleeping on the thin mattress. I stretched my sore limbs and put on a new set of clothes. Naomi was standing by the fire when I finally emerged. Jim was already gone, working I assumed.

"Hello there," Naomi said as I sat down on one of the logs.

I yawned, "Hello."

"I have something I would like to show you." She motioned for me to follow her back into the hut. Once inside she opened one of the wooden boxes and waved me closer. In the bottom of the box there was an old back pack, stuffed full, and crammed underneath Naomi's clothes. She pulled the bag out and handed it to me. "These were the things Lila left behind. I've kept them safe all this time. She would have wanted you to have them." We walked back outside and she continued, "Lila always thought she would come back one day. Deep down I knew she wouldn't, but I kept hoping. Lila was my dearest friend, the closest I came to having a sister, and I failed her."

"How did you fail her?" I asked.

"I knew that man, your father, would ruin her. I tried to warn her, but not hard enough. The minute she got on that plane to London, I felt a hole open in my heart. I knew I'd never see her again." She stopped and wiped her eyes with the back of her hand. For a moment I thought she was crying, but she suddenly shook out of it and said, "I'll leave you alone to look through her things. I have some work to do in the village. Will you be alright here by yourself?"

I nodded. She picked up two big, metal buckets and walked towards the path that led to the village center. I waited until she was far away before I took in a deep breath and slowly opened the back pack.

A small bundle of clothing sat on the top inside the bag. Light colored, thin shirts and shorts my mother must have worn as a teenager that would have been comfortable in the heat. I kept them folded and gently laid them down on the ground next to me. Underneath the clothing, in the bottom of the bag, was a worn copy of *Wuthering Heights* and another journal. Every page of the journal was filled with the same cursive script as the one Mother left for me in London. I put the journal down to save it for last and finished going through the bag. The rest of the items were for survival; an old flashlight with miraculously working batteries, a set of matches, a small knife, and a first aid kit. It was a survival pack, and the last of my mother's possessions.

I repacked the bag and opened the journal. The old journal was much different from the one I found in London. The one Mother wrote for me was a retelling of her biggest mistakes and of her life after she met my Father. The journal from her bag was written when she was younger, before she even met him. The words she wrote were about her life and people in the village. She wrote about Naomi's family after they took her in and of her close relationship with Naomi. She wrote about her friendships with many of the villagers, most of whom I would meet in the weeks to come. There was one name she mentioned regularly, a name I already knew: Ken Saro-Wiwa, the famous Nigerian author. I remembered watching one of his speeches in my history class the year before. He was the man who believed in a free Nigeria with equality for all the people despite their different backgrounds. He was also the man who opposed the oil companies and the corrupted government. I had no idea he and my mother knew each other. He grew up in one of the other Ogoni villages nearby and often visited Mother's village to call on friends and family. Back then he predicted the trouble that oil would cause the Ogoni and as he grew older he dedicated his life to helping better his people.

There was another name, one I didn't recognize, she mentioned often. The name was Soboma George.

She described him as a member of a neighboring community, not the Ogoni, and called him her friend, "despite his many faults." She even compared the two men several times. Ken Saro-Wiwa was a kind man who cared for his people, community, and country, and believed that the written word was the best method to use in resolving the conflicts within the country. George, she described as more violent, interested in retaliation and revenge and a strong, forceful leader.

The end of the journal told about the end of her life in Nigeria; about her decision to marry my father and move to London. She even went so far as to say she loved him when they met and married, unlike how she sounded in the journal written to me. The two journals were a before and an after of her life. I much preferred the "Before" journal when she was happy.

I'm not sure how long I sat there reading the journal, I skimmed through some of it, knowing I would spend plenty of time reading it later, but by the time I finished, Naomi was back carrying the metal buckets

A Rebel Star

she left with. Both buckets were filled to the brim with water and looked extremely heavy, as she set them down next to the fire:

"Did you finish going through Lila's things?" Naomi asked.

"I just finished reading her old journal," I peered at the water in the buckets. They were clear to the bottom with cool, fresh water.

"Learn anything interesting?" Naomi asked curiously.

"I'm not sure yet," I answered, but something about the water distracted me. "Naomi?"

"Yes?"

"Where did you get the water from? It looks so fresh, not like the river water."

She sat down on the log beside me for a rest. "The river water is too polluted to drink. There are

106

many water pumps throughout the village, but most of them are also polluted by the oil. There is only one pump, in the center of the village, which never runs dry and always brings up clean water. At least so far."

"Is that why people are lined up in the middle of the village? For water?"

Naomi nodded.

"There's only one pump for the entire village?"

"Unfortunately, yes. The line is long and every one of us waits our turn in it every day. But we are grateful that we have one at all. I don't know what we would do without it."

"So these two buckets of water are all you have for a whole day?"

Naomi nodded again, "We have a large barrel next to the hut to catch rainwater. We boil it and use it to wash, but these buckets we use for drinking and cooking."

I sat quietly trying to wrap my head around what she was saying. I never thought running water would be an issue when I left London; the idea never crossed my mind. Every day either Naomi or Jim would go into the village, wait in the long line for several hours, and then carry those two heavy buckets all the way back. All of that just so we could survive another day.

The sun was beginning to set when Jim at last came back. I heard him long before I saw him. He came up the river in a small, old, light-blue motor boat. He drove the boat onto the river bank and hopped out, dragging a large net behind him.

"I didn't notice your boat yesterday," I said to Naomi.

She stood over the fire, boiling water in a large pot, "My husband and his family were fishermen. Jim inherited the boat from his father. Now he is the only fisherman left."

"No one else from the village can fish?"

She shook her head, "All of the fishermen gave up after the last oil spill."

"Why?"

"Go and ask Jim, it will give you two something to talk about."

I followed her instructions and joined Jim by his boat. He was taller than I realized when I first met him; he towered over me. His wide friendly smile instantly reminded me of Joseph when he was making us dinner at home. For a moment I felt a pang of regret for not saying goodbye to him and Ruth, and especially Craig, before I left; I was beginning to feel their loss. I sat down on the bow, the front of the boat, and watched Jim work. His hands were big but gentle, as he ran them along the length of the fishing net.

"What are you doing?" I asked him.

He smiled again, "I'm checking the net for holes and loose threads. If even one small thread is loose the entire net could unravel.

"Did you catch anything?"

Sadly he said, "There are no more fish in this part of the river. Not for many miles."

"Why not?"

"Too much pollution. Every time there is an oil spill the land and water here becomes polluted. The water turns black, all the animals—the fish, the birds— they die. The river carries the oil with it, killing everything in its path. It will take many years for this land to heal, but that can only happen if there are no more spills."

"How often do spills happen?"

"No one can predict when they will happen. Sometimes we have several in a year, other times nothing for months. Every time we think it is over another one happens."

I let the information sink in. "Why do you go fishing if there aren't any fish?"

"Because there is always hope."

Chapter 6

The next day when Naomi got up to fetch the daily water, I went with her. People stared at us—and by us I mean me—as we walked down the dirt paths between the huts. The roads and paths were busy with the hustle and bustle of people going about their chores and errands. It was no different, really, than any normal day in London; aside from the fact that it was hotter and much dirtier. My only pair of sneakers was already stained from the dark red, Nigerian dirt. Naomi walked quickly, carrying both buckets by herself despite my offer to help. She told me my company was enough to keep her mind off the work she needed to do. When we reached the center of the village we joined others there at the back of the water line and waited our turn. The line was even longer than the first time I saw it when Danny and Zack left me alone in the village.

People continued to stare at me while we waited, mostly because I was a new face and they were curious, others stared because they remembered my mother. Several people, especially the ones closest to us, introduced themselves to me, shaking my hand, kissing my cheeks, and telling me their names. By the time we were halfway to the water pump I'd learned so many names and met so many people, I was in a daze. I received such a warm welcome from so many complete strangers that it shocked me. Never before in my life had I seen such kindness than I did that day in my new home.

I noticed Danny in the line a long way behind us. I did everything in my power not to look in his direction, but before our turn came I accidentally made eye contact with him. He was standing with a pretty village girl our age, smiling at something she said when I caught his eye. Immediately his smile faltered. We held each other's gaze until the girl standing with him took notice, and waved. Her wave was not a friendly one, more like an acknowledgement or more like a brush off. I turned my head back to the front, where I could finally see the water pump. I didn't have to look back to know that Danny was still watching me.

I walked with Naomi to the water pump every morning after that. Each time we would stand at the back of the line for two to three hours until our turn would come. I would watch Naomi pump water into the buckets and then walk beside her while she carried them home. I offered to help her every time, but she would shrug her shoulders and say it wasn't necessary. I stayed beside her every day watching her as she completed chores around her home and visited some of her close neighbors, bringing some of them food and supplies. Jim went out on the river early every morning, and, every evening he would come back with an empty net. He never gave up hope and I began to admire his perseverance in what appeared to be a lost cause.

By the end of my first week I was tired of sitting around and feeling useless. I got out of bed—and by that I mean I rolled off my straw mattress on the floor— early, my body getting accustomed to its new schedule, and declared that I would be the one to fetch the water that morning, and I would do it by myself.

"You have so many other things you have to do during the day, let me be useful," I told her. "I could save you so much time if you didn't have to wait in that line every day. Please, let me help you."

"Are you sure, Mari? It is a long walk and the buckets are very heavy."

"I've watched you do it a bunch of times now, how hard could it be?" I gave her a big reassuring smile.

"Alright then, but if you have any trouble, come right back and I'll get the water later."

The buckets were kept inside, next to the doorway. I picked them up and quickly realized how hard of a task it was going to be. The buckets were made of thick, strong metal and were plenty heavy on their own without the water. I carried one in each hand, smiled at Naomi again, and took off down the dirt road. It was a little under a mile's walk to get to the end of Naomi and Jim's road, where Danny rudely dropped me off a week before, and then another few minutes to the center of the village.

The line, as usual, stretched around the center and down one of the paths. Everyone in line patiently waited in the heat for their turn, each holding onto the containers they used to collect the water. I say containers, because most people were using large, colorful, plastic bins with no handles. I honestly didn't know how they were able to carry them like that. I stood at the back of the line with my two buckets and began my wait.

I wasn't in line very long when I heard someone behind me say, "I see you made it okay."

I didn't need to see him to know it was Danny, "No thanks to you," I replied.

"You seem to have made it easily enough."

"Easily?" I turned on him. "Are you kidding me? I had to drag that heavy suitcase down a rocky, dirt road, by myself, with no idea where I was. When I asked for directions people started crossing themselves and praying because they thought I was the ghost of my dead mother. It would have taken you five minutes to drive me down that road to Naomi's, but no, instead you ditched me on the side of the road in a place I've never been before, in the middle of a superstitious mob."

"You're right," he confessed. "I should've taken you to Naomi's."

"Bloody right you should have." The line moved forward and I pushed the buckets up with my foot. "You're only apologizing because Naomi told you to."

"I admitted you were right, I never said I was sorry for what I did. You were rude and you deserved it."

"I was rude? You were the one sitting in your seat, judging me and asking questions you didn't have a right to know the answers to."

"I wasn't judging you…"

"Please," I stopped him. "The second you saw me you assumed I was some rich girl on an adventure. You insulted me, even after I answered all of your questions and kept your brother out of jail. I even offered you money to pay for the ride. You're wrong; I didn't deserve it."

"Okay, okay I already admitted I was wrong, but don't pretend that you're any better. You were judging us too. You assumed we were dirty street urchins when you first saw Zack. I watched you sizing us up from that first moment. You're attitude wasn't any better, so don't act like it wasn't partly your fault."

The longer we argued, the further up the line we moved. "You know," I said, "I've been here a week and I'm so sick of hearing your name. Everyone talks about how great Danny is. Danny did this and Danny did that. They all seem to love you, and I don't get it. You're not a great guy, you're just an average jerk."

"It's your turn," he said.

"What?"

He pointed, "It's your turn at the pump, if you're done yelling at me."

"Oh," I pushed the first bucket under the water spout. The well was a simple pump with a lever that had to be lifted up and then pushed back down in order for the water to come out. The metal lever was hot from the sun and burned my hand as I tried to lift it. Pulling the lever up was easy, but pushing it back down was much harder. I gave the lever a good shove and was rewarded with only a small trickle of water that fell into the bottom of my bucket.

"You have to push harder," Danny said from his place in line. The line behind him was long and I could tell people were getting tired of waiting for me.

"I don't need your help," I called back to him. Sweat began to drip from my forehead into my eyes. I wiped it away with the back of my hand and pulled the lever up again. This time I pushed down as hard as I could and was given a large gush of water. It was hard work, but I managed to fill the first bucket to the brim. The real trouble came next; the bucket was so heavy, I couldn't move it. I could feel the people—especially

Danny—watching me and I felt my face growing red in embarrassment. After several minutes of struggling, I maneuvered the first bucket out of the way and put the second bucket under the spout. I knew I didn't have the energy to pump water for the second bucket, but I didn't have a choice.

Danny cleared his throat and I realized he had moved forward while I was moving the bucket. He was standing right next to me with a smirk on his face.

"What?" I said frustrated.

"Move over, I'll do it for you," he said.

"I already told you, I don't need your help."

"You may not *want* it, but you definitely *need* it. And the others want their water sometime today."

"I'm almost done."

"How are you going to carry those buckets if they're both full?"

"I..." he had me there. Danny didn't wait for me to make an excuse. He lifted the first bucket as if it only weighed a couple of pounds, and poured some of the water into the second bucket. He put the first one down pushing me aside so he could finish filling the second. He quickly filled the bucket half way with water so I could carry it and smiled triumphantly at me when he was finished.

"Say thank you," he said grinning.

I ignored him and bent down to pick up my buckets. They were extremely heavy, but I refused to show any more weakness in front of everyone. I took one in each hand and began walking back to Naomi's. When I was far enough away to be forgotten, I stopped to take a break. My arms were weak and the metal handles were digging into my hands. I was never going to make it back. I felt so useless, but I was determined to prove I could do it. I picked the buckets up again and continued my long walk back.

I stopped every few feet to catch my breath and rest my hands. I never gave up, but the further I walked the more frequent my stops became. Each time I rested longer, until I was stopping twice as long as I was moving.

"Will you let me help you, or are you going to argue with me again?" Danny caught up to me carrying two of his own buckets.

"I'm fine," I said not looking at him.

"Okay then, don't say I didn't offer," he walked by me whistling like he was out for a stroll in the park. His buckets were twice as full as mine yet he made them look weightless. I waited for him to disappear from sight so I could put my buckets back down for what felt like the thousandth time. My poor hands were blistered and oozing. They trembled when I tried to pick up the buckets again. I tried a different method. Instead of lifting them, I left the buckets on the ground and tried to drag them. I managed to move the first one several feet and then went back for the second. It took me a while, but I was at last making a little progress. The problem was the water kept splashing and sloshing out of the buckets. I was losing too much water, and wasting water was as bad as any crime.

I couldn't go any further. I didn't want to stop, to give up, but my body refused to keep going. My hands, arms, and shoulders ached from the exercise. I couldn't bring the buckets back to Naomi, and I also couldn't leave them behind. I slumped down on the ground beside them. My face was so drenched in sweat that I didn't notice when I began crying. I leaned my arms across my knees and buried my face in them. I had no plan, no way of getting the buckets back, I was filthy, covered in dust from the road, and I felt utterly defeated. My only hope was that Naomi would get worried after I'd been gone so long and would start looking for me. Otherwise I was going to sit on that dirt road for the rest of my life.

"Mari." It was the first time Danny said my name. He pronounced it with a sigh.

"Just go away," I moaned.

"Come on," he said, "get up." I felt his hands gripping my arms, pulling me up until I was standing on my feet in front of him.

I felt a sense of renewed strength driving me to not look weak in front of him. I pulled my arms away and reached once more for the buckets.

He rolled his eyes, "Give up already, will ya?" He sounded frustrated.

"I can do this on my own," I picked up the buckets and gasped from the pain that shot through my hands. I fought back the tears and tried to move forward, but Danny blocked my way.

"Let me see your hands," he said.

"They're fine."

"Would you stop being so stubborn?" He snatched the buckets away from me, put them down, and grabbed both of my hands. One at a time he turned them over to inspect the damage. His hands were calloused and rough, but gentle. He released me shaking his head, "Those need to be cleaned and bandaged." He picked up my buckets—easily, which was beyond irritation—and said, "Follow me."

"Where are we going?" I asked.

"To take care of those hands."

Danny and his brother lived with their parents in the largest hut in the village. Like all the others, it was a circular mud hut with a palm-frond roof, but the inside was much different from Naomi's and her neighbors. There was a small table with four chairs, several wooden storage boxes like Naomi's, and three straw mattresses made up with blankets and pillows. The floor was newly swept and everything was neatly tucked away in its place. A woman, who could only have been Danny and Zack's mother, was seated at the table.

She smiled and asked, "Who is this?"

"Mom, this is Mari. Mari, this is my mom, Tess." Danny put the buckets down and pushed me ahead of him, further into the hut.

"I've heard a lot about you from my boys," Tess said. "It's so good to finally meet you."

"I can't imagine what you must think of me, if all you've heard comes from Danny and Zack," I said.

Tess laughed a light, bubbly laugh, "I've heard only good things, my dear." She reached out to take my hand and I hesitated. I couldn't shake her hand with my own so blistered and sore. She noticed my hesitation and furrowed her brow looking at my hands. She took one of them and began to inspect it the same way Danny did. "You poor thing, how did this happen?"

"Mari had a little accident today," Danny answered for me as if I was a child.

"I'm afraid my hands aren't used to manual labor," I stated. Danny chuckled behind me and Tess laughed again.

"Come sit down," Tess smiled warmly. "I'll get them cleaned and patched up in no time." I sat down at the end of the table next to Tess, and Danny settled into one of the other empty chairs. It felt so good to sit in a proper chair. I knew I should be grateful for Danny's help, and I was, but I refused to let him know it. I kept my face turned away from him and watched Tess rummage through one of the storage boxes.

"First things first, we have to get those cleaned out," she said sitting back down with a first aid kit. "I'm sorry dear, but this is going to hurt."

Tess used a cloth to rub peroxide over the palms of my hands. The medicine stung as it sizzled, working to clean out any infection. My hands burned. I almost cried out when she applied more of the medicine, but I remembered Danny was watching. I had shown enough weakness for one day. I grit my teeth until Tess was finished cleaning and wrapping my hands.

"There, all done," Tess said tying off the last of the bandages. "Now you're going to have to make sure you keep your hands and the bandages clean at all times. Change the bandages a couple times a day if you need to. An infection is the worst thing that can happen to you here."

"Do you really think these have a chance of becoming infected?" I asked.

"Anything from a paper cut to a serious injury can get infected, and a bad infection could cost you a limb or your life. So, you'll need to be careful and take very good care of your hands. Medical supplies are hard to come by here, you're lucky my sons just brought us a fresh supply. I'll make you a kit to take back to Naomi."

"I don't want to take your supplies, especially if they're so hard to come by," I protested.

"It's okay," Danny said. "Just say, thank you," he snickered.

I looked at Tess again, "Really, I'll be alright. I don't want you to waste them on me."

"Nonsense," she waved me off. "Danny brings back enough to supply most of our village and the..."

"Nearby villages," Danny interrupted her. I witnessed a silent argument between mother and son, which Danny must have won because Tess never finished her thought.

"How long have you lived here?" I asked to change the subject.

"We moved here a little bit before Danny was born. My husband, Barry, worked for one of the oil companies and even when they terminated his employment, we decided to stay."

I perked up a little, "Did you know a woman named Lila?"

Tess smiled, but shook her head, "Only by reputation. She left the village a few weeks before we got here." She paused, "I did meet your father once."

"Really? When?"

"It was a long time ago. He came here to tell Naomi that your mother died. I think he brought her ashes with him."

I nodded, "My mother's will stated she wanted to be cremated and scattered over her favorite place here. We had a service for her that I barely remember, but Father came alone to scatter the ashes. I'm surprised he bothered to visit Naomi."

"Yes, his visit was rather strange, but like I said it was a long time ago."

"Which oil company did your husband work for?" I asked.

"Your Father's," Danny said in a low voice.

"Why was he fired?"

"Because I asked too many of the wrong questions to the wrong people," a man said as he entered the hut. He was a fairly small man, as tall as he was round, with a balding head and a friendly face. "Hello everyone, who might this be?"

"This is Mari," Tess said.

"Ah, the new visitor. Welcome," Barry sat in the last empty chair at the head of the table, but not before he planted a loving kiss on his wife's cheek. Tess beamed at him and grasped his hand on the table. I could not imagine an odder couple. Tess was tall and beautiful, two things her husband was not, but anyone could clearly see how much they loved each other.

"Where is Zack?" Barry asked looking around the room.

"He's off in the village somewhere again. He left after lessons today," Tess answered.

"Do you home school him?" I asked.

"Yes, I teach him and many of the children from our village too."

"Is there no school here?"

"I'm afraid not. One of the closest schools is several miles away and nearly impossible for the children here to get there every day. I was a teacher before we left England, but I am only partly qualified. I do my best to teach them everything they'll need to get by, like reading and simple math, but what they really need is a proper education, which I can't give them."

"Why doesn't the government do anything about it? I mean can't you petition them to build a school?"

"Young lady, those are two of the questions that cost me my job," Barry replied.

"You were fired for asking to help the people that lived here? Why *wouldn't* the government want to help the people? That doesn't make any sense."

"Even if the government did build a school for this village, there would be no money to pay teachers, and volunteers usually go to more destitute areas to help," Tess answered.

"I thought this land was rich with oil."

"It is," Danny said. "It's because of the oil that the government won't help us."

"What do you mean?"

"Nigeria is the fifth largest producer of oil in the world and the government officials will do anything to move it up the list. The River Delta is full of the richest fields in the country and the Ogoni villages sit right on top of one of the best. The government wants to buy this land and drill the oil, so because of that they will never support any new building."

"So why not sell the land and move?"

"Because the money the oil company has offered isn't a fraction of the value of this land. It's nowhere near enough money to help the Ogoni start a new life. Plus, there are over 500,000 Ogoni living in the villages. Where would we all go? We would have to move far away from this land because once they start drilling it will be uninhabitable. And if we travel too far in any direction we will be in another tribe's territory." Danny was animated as he spoke firmly and with conviction. I found, in spite myself, that I enjoyed listening to him speak with passion about issues of the land and people.

"I have a son that is too free with his opinions and another who is never in the same place twice," Barry laughed clapping a hand on Danny's back.

"Does Zack really run off that often?" I asked.

"He's constantly visiting people in the different villages. Sometimes he even finds his way into Port Harcourt on his own, though I'm not sure how. I don't care where he goes as long as he stays away from the rebel camps."

"Barry…" Tess warned her husband.

"Rebel camps?" I interrupted.

Danny cleared his throat, "There are a couple of camps nearby. They make demands of the oil company and the government to better this place, which has given them the label 'rebel.'"

"And what happens when the company or the government doesn't meet their demands?" I asked already knowing the answer.

"They sabotage the company. Blow up pipelines, cut the power to the rigs, whatever they have to do to be heard."

"That's enough now," Barry stopped him. "We don't want to frighten the poor girl, she's only just arrived."

"I'm not frightened," I told them. "I'm interested actually. I've never understood the politics of my father's business."

The sky grew dark as we spoke. Danny stood up from the table and said, "Come on Mari, I'll walk you back and then go look for my brother."

I stood to follow him, but before I left the hut I stopped and thanked Tess for taking care of my hands. She handed me a small package of medical supplies to give to Naomi and both Tess and her husband invited me back. They were kind people—loving and warm—so different from their wild and opinionated sons. Danny carried the water buckets for me and took the lead down the dirt road. I walked a few paces behind him, each of his long strides equaling about two of mine. We were silent, the only sounds were our footsteps and the water sloshing in the buckets. Almost everyone was indoors, the last of the light fading away.

We bumped into a frantic Jim on one of the paths. Naomi had been worried and sent him out to find me. He said he looked everywhere in the village but there was no sign of me anywhere. Someone finally told him that they saw me with Danny. He was on his way to Danny's hut to check on me when we ran into him. He was so relieved to find me safe and even more relieved to see I was with Danny. Jim took the buckets from Danny and thanked him for his help. I was glad that I wasn't going to have to walk the whole way back with Danny; I much preferred Jim's company.

Before he walked away, Danny said, "I need to borrow the truck again tomorrow, if that's okay."

Jim nodded, "The keys are under the seat."

"Thanks Jim," the two young men shook hands.

"Be careful Danny, you know you can't trust them."

"I know, believe me."

He turned to leave and I couldn't help but feel like there was something more I needed to say to him. I called out his name and he turned to face me again, a smile lighting up his entire face. I stood there looking like a fool, trying to find something, anything to say.

"Just say thank you," he told me with a smile as though he knew I was struggling for my words. He didn't wait for a reply, but turned and walked towards the village center.

"Thank you," I whispered to his back.

Chapter 7

I wanted to go someplace new. A place where I could think without the fear of being found. I bought a bus ticket out of Port Harcourt and rode an entire day to Calabar, Nigeria, near the Cameroon border. I hiked into the jungle and found the most amazing waterfalls. I'd heard they were beautiful, but I never imagined this. I'm sitting near the edge of a cliff over-looking seven different waterfalls all converging at the same place. Everything is bright green and covered in mist from the falls. There's even a rainbow in the mist.

I've been sitting here for a while, listening to the water as it crashes into the pool below. I've thought of climbing down there and finding a safe place to swim downstream, --it is so hot today!—but for now I only want to listen. The jungle is all around me, the water is deafening, yet I've never felt more at peace than I do right now.

I didn't tell anyone I was leaving. I know that Naomi and her family will worry if I don't go back soon, but I'm not ready to leave yet. I've been thinking about my parents a lot lately. I turned 18 this year, which means they've been gone for nine years. Half of my life I've lived without Mum and Dad. I'm so grateful to Naomi's family for taking me in for these long, nine years, but I miss my parents.

This week is the anniversary of their deaths. I went to visit their graves, like I always do, but this time I felt like I needed to do something more. They're buried in the little cemetery in our village. I feel bad about that. I've decided I never want to be buried...anywhere. I don't want to be squeezed into a little wooden box and buried beneath six feet of dirt. I want to be free. My family was from London, but Nigeria is my home. I want to roam free across the land, scattered in the wind above this beautiful place. I want my ashes to be forever a part of Nigeria.

I think I'll stop writing now. I want to fall asleep to the sounds of the water and the jungle, and then I'll go back. I don't want Naomi's family to worry for too long.

January 1993

"Naomi?"

"Yes, Mari?" Naomi was busy weaving a basket out of palm fronds.

"My mother mentions a place in her journal where seven waterfalls meet in the middle of the jungle. She talks about it a lot and I think it's the place where Father scattered her ashes. Do you know where that is?"

"I do," Naomi answered. "Agbokim Falls, near the Cameroon border. It was your mother's favorite place. She went there often to be alone, but I went with her once or twice."

"Can we go? I would really like to see it."

"Of course we can go, child. It is about a day's journey from here. We can take the truck and camp there for a couple of days."

"Could we leave tomorrow?" I asked excitedly.

"Not tomorrow, no."

"Why not?"

"Why the rush, girl? The waterfalls are not going anywhere. Tomorrow is a very special day here. Tomorrow is Ogoni Day."

"Ogoni Day? You have a day?"

"This will be our first one. Ken Saro-Wiwa himself, along with MOSOP, has organized it."

"What is MOSOP?"

"It is the 'Movement for the Survival of the Ogoni People,' an organization Ken Saro-Wiwa and several of our leaders founded three years ago. Tomorrow the Ogoni, as a nation, are going to stand together in protest against the government and all others who oppose us."

"Meaning the oil company," I said.

Naomi nodded, "It is going to be a peaceful protest. I believe Ken Saro-Wiwa will be leading it himself."

I waited a few seconds before I said, "Maybe I should stay here tomorrow."

"Nonsense, why would you wish to do that?"

"Because the protest is against my father's company, people might be angry with me if I show up. They'll hate me."

"You are too dramatic. The company does not belong to your father."

"No, but he runs it..."

"And," she cut me off, "...no one will hate you."

"My father runs the company that's been stealing and destroying their lands, how could they not hate me? I hate me. The more I see of this place, the more I hate myself for the life I used to live."

Naomi dropped her work onto the ground and seized my face with one of her hands. Her fingers squeezed my cheeks, "Don't you ever say that again.

You must never hate yourself for the things your father has done; they are not your fault. The people here know that and they do not blame you. They do not hate you or your father, they only hate what has happened to their homes and lands, but you have nothing to do with that. Do you understand me?"

"Yes ma'am."

She released my face and placed her hands on my shoulders. She held me there at arm's length for a moment, her eyes distant, and her mind wandering to a different time in her past. "You are the spitting image of your mother." She let go and resumed her work, "Come to Ogoni Day with us tomorrow and see for yourself what it's all about. We will visit the waterfalls in a few days, alright?"

I nodded my head, "Okay."

That night I fell asleep dreaming of the waterfall my mother described. I could feel the mist on my face as I listened to the sound of water rushing over a cliff and crashing into a pool below. I could see and smell the jungle all around me. As I dreamed I imagined the faces of the grandparents I had never met. I imagined how they looked and what their voices would have sounded like. Mother mentioned their graves in her journal entry. They were buried somewhere within the village; such a short distance away. It was strange; I never really gave my mother's parents much thought. I never knew my mother, so why would I think about her parents? She wasn't even around long enough to tell me stories about them. I traveled all the way from London to learn about my mother's past, but why stop with just her? I awoke with a newly discovered need to know everything about my grandparents, not least the reason why they moved to Nigeria in the first place.

I found Naomi and Jim first thing in the morning and told them I would meet them at the celebrations later. Naomi asked if I wanted her or Jim to show me where the graves were, but I told her that I would rather go alone. She understood and told me where I could meet them later. The day was beautiful, bright and sunny and hot, but with a light breeze. I still couldn't get used to the weather, it was early January and I was wearing shorts and a t-shirt. In London I would have been wearing a winter coat with hat and gloves. It was so hot, but I preferred it to the dark, rainy, London days.

I was walking in the opposite direction as everyone else on the paths. The villagers accepted me as a part of normal life, but there were still several who kept their eyes on me, wary of a stranger in their village. I moved through the people as inconspicuously as I could, always yielding the right-of-way to others. Danny and Zack were among the moving crowd walking towards me.

Zack noticed me, waved, and shouted, "Mari! You're going the wrong way! You're gonna miss all the fun!"

I shouted back, "I'll be there later. Save me a good spot!"

"You got it!"

They disappeared down the path with everyone else and I continued walking until I found the quiet little cemetery. Small, wooden crosses were planted in the ground in almost perfect rows, completely opposite of the large, elaborate headstones in the old, London cemeteries. I walked among the graves looking for my grandparent's names on the crosses. They were in the very back row, the only two graves with stones instead of crosses. Their headstones, engraved in the traditional way, were barely taller than my ankles. I knelt down in front of them and ran my hand over the names of the family I would never know.

"Hello," I whispered knowing they couldn't hear me. There was something peaceful about the silence of this graveyard. I was completely alone; the roads and paths empty, the villagers all gone to join the celebrations.

Curiosity about Ogoni Day is what pulled me away from my grandparent's graves. It wasn't hard to find the throng of people gathered in the middle of the village. Finding Naomi and Jim was an entirely different matter. I looked for them, but gave up after a few minutes. Many people were packed together in the small area, cheering loudly with excitement. Members of MOSOP—the organization Naomi mentioned the day before—took their turns standing in front of the crowd and speaking about the forms of oppression the Ogoni were living with. They were protesting against more than just an oil company taking and destroying their lands, they were peacefully fighting for civil rights within their country.

I missed the opening speeches while I was in the cemetery and from the back of the crowd I could barely hear what the speakers were saying. After the last speaker, who I still couldn't understand, but who seemed to inspire the crowd, we started to move. The better word to use is march. The people began their march of protest, cheering and singing and waving picket signs down the road, out of the village, into the open. I got swept up by the rest of them, forced forward by the momentum of the crowd. My feet kept pace with the others, and my hands clapped in time to their singing. I was a part of something bigger than myself, something both empowering and exciting. *The whole world must be seeing this,* I thought. *Father must be watching.* The thought of Father knowing that I was taking part in a protest against him made my feet move faster and my hands clap louder. Every second I spent in the crowd was a second that I knew we were making history. The crowd numbered over 300,000—the largest number of people ever to move in protest against the oil industry. My face was only one amongst them; easily lost and completely unimportant on its own. If my mother were still alive she would have marched alongside them, the people she loved so much, cheering and singing along with the crowd. I closed my eyes for a moment and could picture her standing beside me.

The march brought us to each of the four major Ogoni villages where, one at a time, more speeches were delivered and more people joined the march. When we stopped in the last village, Zack found me squeezed in the middle of all the people and he pulled me up to the front where he was standing with members from our village. Danny, of course, was with him along with the pretty girl I often saw him with. She told me her name was Natalie when I joined them, she smiled and was friendly, but she eyed me suspiciously the same way Danny had the first day we met. From the first rows of people I could clearly make out the speakers' faces and the words they were saying.

Ken Saro-Wiwa was the last to deliver his speech in every village. His words rallied the people to march in each new place, but it wasn't until I stood in the front with Zack and the others that I was finally able to hear and understand his words. He caught my eye and a look of recognition crossed his face. Throughout his speech he would briefly take his eyes off mine to skim the audience, but each time they returned to me.

"Why does he keep looking at you like that?" Zach whispered to me.

There was only one reason I could think of, "He knew my mother," I told him.

Ken Saro-Wiwa told his people that they would not fight against their oppressors. Violence would bring them nothing but violence. Adopting the methods of other great men before him, men like Martin Luther King, Jr. from America, and Gandhi of India, Ken Saro-Wiwa and his people would march free of any form of violence. Every year on the same day they were to gather and march, in order to show the world that they would gain their victory:

"...over the evil forces of marginalization, unconscionable military brutality against defenseless and law-abiding citizens, untold oppression, economic deprivation, environmental despoliation, and criminal

neglect by the Nigerian state and their corporate agents..."[2]

The people were not to fight; they were to dance.

"Dance your anger and your joys

Dance the military guns to silence

Dance their dumb laws to the dump

Dance oppression and injustice to death

Dance the end of Shell's ecological war of 30 years

Dance my people for we have seen tomorrow

And there is an Ogoni Star in the sky!"[3]

The last words he spoke were as if they were being said to me personally. His hands were raised above his head in triumph and while the crowd cheered

[2] *See Bibliography*

[3] *See Bibliography*

wildly, we stood holding each other's gaze. I no longer clapped or cheered; I only stared at the man who could not stop staring at me. Another man, a member of MOSOP, took Ken Saro-Wiwa's place in front of the people, congratulating them on making the first official Ogoni Day a success. The crowd continued their cheering, but Danny, Natalie, and Zack did not. Zack looked at me in awe of what he witnessed. Natalie watched me, her arms crossed, with more suspicion and perhaps even a bit of contempt. Danny seemed confused. He looked at me differently as if deciding what to make of me.

The crowd began to disperse slowly, due to its size. Some began the walk back to their own villages; others started celebrating by doing exactly what they had been told to do; dance. Groups were circled together dancing and singing, some even had drums. Their music could be heard for miles around as they played for the rest of the day and into the night.

I noticed Ken Saro-Wiwa mingling with his fellow speakers and watched as he and a couple of others disappeared into one of the huts. I followed them and stood beside the small window carved into the hut's rounded, mud wall. I listened to the voices speak with excitement of their success. I even dared to peek inside and saw three men sitting at a small table not unlike the one in Tess and Barry's hut.

"Are you going to continue spying on me from the window or would you like to come in through the door as a guest?" Ken Saro-Wiwa's voice called out to me. I walked around to the doorway and cautiously entered.

"I am sorry," I said. "I did not mean to spy. I was..."

"Curious," he finished my sentence. "Please, come in and sit. Would you like a cup of tea?"

I nodded and sat down on the chair across from him. One of the men left the hut and returned with a cup of tea. English tea, I noticed, as fine as the tea I would drink with Kirstin at the Ritz. The man also brought a pipe filled with tobacco and handed it to Ken Saro-Wiwa.

"Ah," he said as he took his first long drag on the pipe and slowly exhaled the smoke. "I hope you don't mind if I smoke. There is nothing more soothing than a fresh pipe full of tobacco after a long day on your feet speaking to crowds. Give me my pipe and a delicious home-cooked meal every day and I am a happy man."

I didn't know how to respond so I said, "The speech you gave today was brilliant."

"Thank you." He took another pull on his pipe. "Now I believe you might have a few questions for me, am I right?"

"I'm not sure what to ask. You knew my mother, her name was..."

"Lila. A beautiful, kind woman raised in the villages by our people. I knew her well, although I did not spend as much time with her as I would have liked to."

"You recognized me because of her."

"I must admit you gave me a bit of a start. There is no difference between you and your mother. I knew you immediately. I had heard rumors of the 'returned daughter' of the Ogoni, but I did not realize how much you would look like her."

"They are calling me a 'returned daughter?'" I asked surprised. "How can I be 'returned'? I've never been here before."

"You have brought your mother back for the people that remember her. Though, I think they will be calling you something else after today."

"You spoke the last words of your speech as though they were meant for me. You said, 'We have

158

seen tomorrow and there is an Ogoni Star in the sky.' What did you mean?"

"The poem was meant to move our people. If we continue on this path of non-violent protesting, the world will soon have to listen. And when the world finally sees what is happening in this country they will be forced to put a stop to it. Only then will our people be allowed to rise; to reach for the stars." He paused to sip his tea and take another pull on his pipe. "Of course, I did not realize that we would already have a star among us, when I planned to give my speech." He looked pointedly at me.

"Me?"

"You do not know then. I thought as much. Your name Marienela," he pronounced each syllable slowly and smoothly, "means star."

My name. He knew the meaning of my name. "Why did my mother choose this name?" I asked him. "Was it your idea?"

"It was not. The literal meaning is 'Rebel Star' and was suggested by someone else, but I will not tell you who. I have a feeling you will meet him on your own soon enough. Know that he is no friend of mine and is the reason I cannot decide if your presence here is a blessing or a curse for our people."

"You keep saying 'our' people."

"Do you not claim them then? Do you not love them? Have you not chosen to live as one of them?" Asked Ken Saro-Wiwa.

"I..." I stammered. "I haven't given it much thought really. I do love them and I am so grateful to them for taking me in; only, I do not know if they would wish to claim me as their own, given my background. I don't want to offend them."

His smile widened as he leaned back in his chair. "Oh I think they already have. There are two listening at the window even now." I looked towards the window and back to Ken Saro-Wiwa, who was laughing. "Go on, have a look," he told me.

I stood up and peered outside the window. Danny and Zack were leaning against the wall of the hut, each with the same look of guilt written across their faces.

"You followed me?" I asked Danny sharply.

"No, Zack followed you and I followed him," Danny answered.

"You may invite them in," Ken Saro-Wiwa called out. Danny and Zack entered and the three of us stood before the three members of MOSOP. The two other men in the room spoke little; although they were not unfriendly and saw that the conversation was really between me and Ken Saro-Wiwa. He greeted both boys warmly and offered them tea, which they refused.

"We can't stay too much longer. I promised our parents we wouldn't be home late," Danny said.

"And yet, you were content to sit outside my window and listen to my private conversations. Interesting," he let out a great puff of smoke. "You know, there are only two types of men who follow a woman: those that are in love and those who do not yet know they are in love."

"You mean...you think I...that's not possible...I..." Poor Danny was speechless. Zack and the other men in the hut snickered causing Danny's face to turn red.

"Danny and I have no feelings for each other, I can assure you," I said and Danny nodded furiously in agreement.

"I see then, that you fall into the latter category. Very well, all will be revealed in time. This boy, my young star," he said addressing me, "will lead you to the answers that you seek; do not discount him yet. My advice to you Danny is to tread very carefully down the path you are on. You know of what I speak."

Danny nodded again.

"You two have a long journey ahead of you, I can sense it. You will have to learn to trust each other. Personally, I am leaving soon for my home in London. It was a pleasure to meet you before I left, Marienela. Your mother would have been proud of you, as much as I'm sure your father is disappointed, though I do not think you care about his opinion."

"No sir," I answered and smiled. "Can I ask you one more thing?"

He nodded.

"If you live in London, how come you never came to visit?"

"I could not be seen at the household of my enemy, could I? You and I did meet once."

"We did?"

"In the months before Lila died. You were very small and I happened, by accident, to meet all of you— you, Lila, your brother, your nanny, and your cook—in the park. It was a chance meeting, the last time I ever saw Lila and the first time I met you. I was so very glad to find that Ruth and Joseph were a help to her, especially near the end."

"You knew Ruth and Joseph?"

"Of course! Who do you think recommended them to your mother?"

I nearly laughed out loud. The people who raised me and Craig in our mother's place were hand-picked by her friend, Ken Saro-Wiwa. He had a better hand in raising us than our own father. The thought was comforting and exciting at the same time. I kept picturing Father's face, if he ever found out the truth, and the thought made me smile. Danny and Zack turned to leave; our time with Ken Saro-Wiwa- nearly over, and I stood up to join them. It was only as I was about to leave that I decided to say one more thing.

"The world knows," I told him.

He looked at me strangely, "Knows what?"

"The truth about what's happening here. We learned about Nigeria in my history class. My teacher recorded one of your speeches and made us all watch. He said it would take a long time for things to get better, but that they *would* get better." I paused. "The world knows."

Ken Saro-Wiwa said nothing in response, merely nodded his head to me and raised his pipe in farewell.

"That was..."

"Amazing!" I finished for Danny.

There were people standing outside the hut when we left, all waiting for their own chance to catch a glimpse of Ken Saro-Wiwa. They asked us all kinds of questions when we left the hut. I overheard someone whisper, "That's the girl he was looking at during his speech."

Another asked, "Are you sure?"

"She's the only white girl I've seen all day."

Once we pushed our way through the small group at the hut, we rejoined the larger crowd from earlier. There were several people dancing in front of us, who tried to get me to join them, but we kept moving. We didn't stop until we were completely away from everyone else.

"I can't believe that just happened!" Danny exclaimed.

"Neither will anyone else back home," Zack said.

"Oh they'll believe us," Danny said. "We're bringing proof back with us."

"What proof?" I asked.

"We're bringing back a Star," he said stopping. Both boys were staring at me with wide grins, as if waiting for me to say something.

"I don't know the way back," was all I could manage.

Danny stepped forward, "Then we'll walk...together."

Danny and I may not have liked each other, but we were going to have to put our differences aside. There was a long journey ahead of us and we were going to do it...together.

Chapter 8

Zack was wrong; as it turned out everyone in the village believed our story. In fact we were asked to repeat it many times for the people who wanted to hear all about our private conversation with Ken Saro-Wiwa. I wanted to leave some of the details out, especially those regarding my mother and my name, but Zack was too excited to hold anything back. Naomi and Jim were the only ones I personally told the full story to and they forced me to retell it several times over, wanting to learn everything they could about the man who was inspiring their people. The only person who didn't seem very excited for us was Danny's friend Natalie, but I paid her no attention.

For the next few days, I continued my routine of following Naomi around, assisting occasionally with her chores and keeping her company. She even taught me how to weave a basket, which took a while to become skilled at it. I viewed the village and people with a new viewpoint, and began to call them my own. Wherever I went in the village people smiled and greeted me and called me by my full name: Marienela. Rebel star. Only, I felt I had done nothing to earn such a title.

With a new determination to prove that I could be as strong as my name implied, I attempted to retrieve water for Naomi again. I told her that there was nothing she could do to stop me and that I was absolutely resolved to doing this completely on my own. I left no room for argument. After my first failure, I knew that I was not yet strong enough to carry both water buckets, so instead I woke up extremely early in the morning hoping to beat the worst of the line, and only carried one bucket with me. Because the line was not as long I was able to fill the bucket faster. I wrapped a cloth around the handle to prevent myself from getting anymore blisters, and occasionally switched hands to keep them from wearing out. I brought the water to Naomi and took the second bucket back to the line, which had grown in my absence. I waited in the line, filled the bucket, and carried it back to Naomi. I repeated the process the next day and every day after that until I was strong enough to carry both buckets at once. The villagers noticed the change in me and began to show their approval of me by including me in their conversations while we waited together in line. Every day I walked by Danny as he waited his turn in the line behind me, and every day I could feel his eyes staring at me as I went.

I felt myself growing stronger and stronger as time went by. Naomi and Jim kept promising to take me to Agbokim Falls, the place that my mother loved so much, but the more I thought about it the more I realized it was a journey that I needed to make on my own. One early morning while Naomi and Jim were still sleeping, I quietly packed some clothes into my mother's old back pack. Using a stick, I drew a note in the dirt for Naomi, in a place by the fire where I knew she would see it.

Went to the Falls. Be back in a few days.

♡

Mari

I had no plan, only a destination: Agbokim Falls. Following the same path I knew my mother took all those years past, I walked down the main road and hitched a ride into Port Harcourt. I climbed into the bed of a pick-up truck with three other men and a woman who were all on their way to work in the city. We drove by the Borikiri Market where vendors were setting up their stands for the day, and on into the center of the city. From there I walked to the International Airport, where the bus terminal was located. I bought a bus ticket to Calabar in the Cross Rivers State. The only credit card I brought with me was supposed to be used only for an emergency. In using it to purchase the bus ticket I knew my father would easily be able to locate me. I didn't care anymore. There was nothing he could do to me. I had made my decision and we both had to live with it. There was no way I would ever live under the same roof with him again.

My timing was perfect. Within an hour of arriving at the terminal the bus was ready to depart. It was a white, coach bus with comfortable seats and a broken air conditioner. I sat in a window seat almost exactly in the middle of the bus, and watched the rest of the passengers as they boarded. A woman with two small children and a baby sat in the rows behind me. The baby was crying, the little boy kicked the back of my seat, and the mother scolded both of her children. An older man in a straw hat smiled and sat down in the aisle across from me. A middle aged couple took the seats in front of me, and a group of teenagers took up the last two rows in the back. There were several more passengers sitting in the front of the bus that I couldn't see. The seat beside me remained empty, so I propped my legs up, placed the back pack beside them, and leaned my back against the window.

The ride was going to be a long one; nearly a whole day's worth of driving. After the first couple of hours, I realized I should have eaten a snack while I was in the city. I skipped breakfast in my rush to leave and I was paying for it. My stomach was screaming for food. I wouldn't have been surprised if the whole bus could hear it. Perhaps they did hear because the little girl sitting behind me offered me a banana, which I thankfully accepted. The mother smiled and whispered something like "Good girl," to her daughter in their own language. The banana was delicious, but anything would have been since I was so hungry. After that, I didn't mind as much when the little boy kicked my seat.

As we rode along, the land changed from what I vaguely remembered from my arrival to completely different ones I had never seen before. In reality, we still were not that far away from the Ogoni villages, only about an hour, when we happened upon a road block. I sat up in my seat, along with everyone else, and tried to see ahead. From my angle all I could make out was a couple of military jeeps parked alongside the road.

The driver stopped the bus and opened the door so he could speak with the soldiers. One of the soldiers stepped into the bus, carrying his automatic rifle in front of him. He argued with the driver in voices too low for the rest of us to hear. The other passengers were growing nervous. Something felt wrong about the road block and the way the soldier was acting. I took my passport out of my back pack and slipped it into my pocket along with the knife and the lighter my mother left behind. The knife was too big for my pocket especially with its leather cover, so I slid into the waistband of my shorts. It wasn't comfortable, but for some reason I knew I didn't want to leave it behind.

When I was finished hiding all the important things in my shorts, the soldier shouted, "Everybody Out! Now!"

We hurried off the bus, leaving our belongings behind. I noticed the older man who sat across from me struggling to make the last step off the bus, which was several inches too high above the ground. I gave him my hand and helped him down. He smiled at me gratefully and we lined up next to each other with the rest of the passengers. That was when I recognized the man in charge.

The Captain from Borikiri Market, the one I bribed to get Zack out of trouble, was the officer in charge of the road block. He paced in front of the passengers and I ducked my head praying he wouldn't recognize me. I escaped him once; I was sure it wouldn't happen again. He questioned the passengers one by one, down the line, repeating the same questions over and over. He was looking for information about a group of rebels, their plans, and their location. The passengers answered him in few words, as respectfully as possible, never making eye contact with him out of fear. The Captain stopped in front of the old man and made him step forward out of the line.

"Where are the rebel camps?" The Captain asked.

The old man did not answer. He kept his eyes looking straight ahead, his chin high. His demeanor gave me the feeling that he had the information the soldiers were looking for. The Captain stood in front of him, their faces only inches apart, and asked again, "Where are the rebels hiding?"

The old man still remained silent. The Captain became angry and using the back of his hand he slapped the old man across his face. The blow knocked the old man onto the ground, and two of the soldiers picked him up and held him between them. Unable to stay quiet, I rushed forward and placed myself between the Captain and the old man.

"How dare you hit a defenseless old man," I said, courage and adrenaline flowing through me.

"I remember you," the Captain said pointing a finger in my face. "This is not the first time you have come between me and justice. I think this time will end differently."

"You call justice terrorizing innocent people, asking them questions you know they don't have the answers to?"

"Maybe I should be asking you the questions then," he waved his hand and his soldiers let go of the old man. He returned to his place in the line, his face already showing signs of a bruise. "Where are the rebels?" The Captain asked me.

"I don't know," I answered defiantly. The Captain raised his hand and I closed my eyes as he brought the back of it against my face. The force of it did not knock me to the ground as it had the old man, but the entire right side of my face stung with pain. I felt a wetness trickle from my lip and wiped blood away with the back of my hand. I ignored the pain and straightened myself up so that I was standing face to face with the Captain. My fearlessness brought a wicked grin to his face. He moved closer, so close that I could feel his breath on my cheek.

"I believe you know more than you want to tell," he said in a hushed voice. "Perhaps a few hours at my office will bring it out of you."

His men moved to grab me, but before they could even touch me, gunfire exploded from the road. Three jeeps, full of men with automatic weapons, drove up the road and opened fire on the soldiers. I quickly dropped to the ground, caught in the middle of a gunfight between the rebels and the soldiers. The other passengers were yelling and running, some were on the ground like me, others ran into the cover of the nearby jungle. I used my elbows and knees to propel myself forward, keeping as low to the ground as I could. Bullets ricocheted off the ground all around me, barely missing me, and throwing dirt into my face.

I reached the edge of the road when the old man from the bus decided to turn back for me. He was also crawling, but he didn't keep himself low enough. A stray bullet—whether from a rebel or a soldier, I would never know—pierced his stomach and the old man collapsed onto the ground. I crawled to him quickly and rolled him over onto his back. There was blood everywhere. I found the wound on his belly and, using all the medical knowledge I obtained from watching old action movies, I pressed my weight against the opening in an effort to stop the bleeding. It was no use, but I kept trying, my hands becoming slippery in his blood. He lifted a hand to grasp mine. I looked at his face and saw blood dripping from his mouth.

"Run," he spat, "run." His hand dropped to the ground as he let out his last breath.

"I'm sorry." I could feel tears stinging my eyes. "I'm so sorry."

I left his body lying on the side of the road, and pushed myself forward as hard as I could until I was almost at the edge of the trees. *Keep moving,* I told myself, *all you have to do is keep moving, you're almost there.* Then someone's hands were grabbing me, picking me up off the ground, and pulling me towards the jungle. I couldn't see whose hands they were and out of fear I kicked and punched at the person trying to free myself.

"Ow," a voice said as my elbow connected with flesh. "Mari, it's me."

Danny.

He helped me get my footing and, no questions asked, we ran together into the jungle. Danny led me by the hand deep into the jungle until the sound of gunfire and men shouting faded into the distance. We stopped at the edge of a river and I slumped down, exhausted, on a large rock.

"Where are you hurt?" Danny knelt down in front of me inspecting every inch of my body, desperately looking for any injuries. The only thing going through my mind was the old man's face as he used his dying breath to tell me to leave him behind and save myself. "Where is all this blood coming from? Mari, where are you hurt?"

I shook my head, "It's not my blood," I said quietly. My hands and clothing were smeared with blood from trying to help the old man. I moved to the edge of the water and tried to wash my hands. The blood clouded the water and drifted away with the current. I scrubbed and scrubbed my skin raw, but no matter how much I scrubbed I couldn't seem to get it all off.

"Mari, it's gone now," Danny told me taking my hands so I was forced to stop. "You've got it all," he said. The tears came on their own before I even realized it. Danny let me lean my head on his shoulder while I sobbed. He placed one of his hands on the back of my head and whispered soothing reassurances, "Shh, come on now, everything's okay, you're going to be fine."

" I tried so hard to help him," I said.

"There was nothing you could've done," he told me.

Danny was wearing a white, button-up shirt over a black tank top. He ripped a piece of the white shirt off, dipped it in the water and held it against the right side of my face where I could feel a bruise forming. The cold water was soothing against the swelling and I leaned further into Danny's hand. He dipped the shirt back into the water and wiped away some of the dirt and blood from my face. He gave me the piece of shirt to keep pressed against the bruise to help with the swelling, helped me sit back down on the rock, and then he turned on me.

"What were you thinking, running off on your own like that? You could've been killed!" He yelled at me. "This country is seconds from breaking out into a civil war. It is run by a military regime filled with corrupt leaders, and is crawling with all sorts of rebel groups. It's dangerous for the locals, never mind the tourists. And you..." he paused to look at me, "do you have any idea how valuable you'd be as a hostage...for either side?"

"I wasn't thinking," I said.

"No, you weren't."

"How did you know where to find me?" I asked.

"I saw you riding by Borikiri Market in the back of a truck. I assumed Naomi and Jim didn't know where you were because they never would have let you go by yourself."

"So you followed me again?" I added.

He sighed, "I thought you were leaving. I watched you walk into the airport and I thought you were going back to England. I wanted to know for sure, in case Naomi and Jim went looking for you. I searched for you inside the airport, but couldn't find you anywhere. I was about to give up when I finally saw you getting on a bus. I knew the roads were going to be dangerous today, so I decided to follow the bus."

"Oh, so you were just following me for my protection," I said sarcastically.

"Alright, I'll admit I was curious," He said. "I saw the road block from a distance and was able to pull off the road and hide the truck. Then I hiked through the jungle, using the trees for cover, and stopped near the road block so I could see what the soldiers were going to do. I saw you step in front of the old man and take a hit from the Captain. I heard the rebels coming up the road and waited for the right time to run out and help you."

He finished his story and I said, "You followed me all the way from Port Harcourt and watched as I got questioned, beaten, and shot at before you came to help me?"

"I came to help as soon as I could," he paused. "Where were you going anyway?"

"None of your business," I snapped.

"Hey I just saved your life, I'm entitled to some answers."

"Saved my life? I was doing just fine without you, I was practically all the way to safety by the time you showed up."

Danny perked up as if he heard something in the jungle, but I ignored him, "Where do you get off anyway?"

"Shh," he told me looking all around us.

"Don't 'shh' me. You know, it's not normal behavior to follow people around all the time…"

"Be quiet," he said again.

"…It's really starting to creep me out."

In one, swift movement, Danny cupped a hand over my mouth and dragged me further into the trees where we couldn't be seen. Two rebel men emerged from nowhere, carrying their guns at the ready. They stopped by the side of the river, scanning the trees. One of them reached down and drank a handful of the water. Danny took his hand off my mouth and put a finger to his lips signaling me to keep quiet. I didn't move an inch while we waited for the men to leave. When they finally disappeared, I let out a breath I wasn't aware I was holding. I stayed planted until Danny said it was safe for us to move.

"Look, I'm sorry that I grabbed you, and that I followed you, and for anything else you're angry about. I'm going to need you to trust me now, okay? We can't go back to the road, it's not going to be safe again for a while, which means we can't get to the truck. I have a plan, but you're going to have to trust me and listen to everything I tell you. Do you think you can do that?"

I nodded.

"Alright then," he started walking into the jungle and I followed after him. "There are two different kinds of rebels in this country. The ones who are fighting for a cause—the most notorious of which are a group called the Outlaws—and the ones who fight for the sake of fighting. Both kinds are ruthless and dangerous."

"Where are we going?" I asked.

He turned and smiled, "To see the Outlaws."

★♦★

The Outlaw's rebel camp was nearly a day's journey on foot. We began our trek around mid-day, and because it would be dark early, we were forced to spend the night in the jungle. We stopped as the first lights began to fade and found ourselves a comfortable and safe place to spend the night.

"I wasn't exactly prepared for a night in the jungle when I left this morning," Danny said. "We'll have to make do without a fire; I don't have any matches."

"You mean the 'Amazing' Danny can't make a fire with his bare hands?" I mocked.

"I'm still working on that," he replied and we both laughed.

"How about with this then?" I tossed him the lighter from my pocket.

"Now *that* I can do," he said. "Why do you have a lighter in your pocket?"

"I didn't know what was going to happen at the road block, so I stashed a few valuables into my pockets before I got off the bus." Then, seeing his expression, I added, "Don't look so surprised, I'm a lot smarter than you give me credit for."

"I'll be sure to keep that in mind," he said.

I helped him gather fire wood for the night, never straying too far from his sight. I felt safer with him close by. Not that I would admit it to him. He knew how to survive and to distrust him would have been a foolish act on my part if I wanted to survive. We set up our little camp next to an old, fallen log and started the fire a few feet in front of it. I sat down with my back against the log, my feet straight out in front of me, and watched Danny light the fire.

"This will keep the animals away," he said as the flames rose up. He sat down beside me and used a long stick to poke at the burning wood.

"I was going to Agbokim Falls," I told him, finally answering his question. "Have you ever been there?"

He shook his head, "I've heard of it before, but I've never seen it." He added, "I've heard it's beautiful."

"That's where my mother's ashes were scattered. It was her favorite place. That's why I wanted to go alone."

We sat quietly for a long time. The jungle turned black around us as night fell. There were all kinds of sounds coming out from the trees. The nocturnal animals began waking up and searching for food. Despite my best efforts, I couldn't keep myself from imagining all the different kinds of animals that could jump out at any moment and try to eat us. The thought was terrifying and kept me wide awake.

As if he could read my mind, Danny said, "You should try to sleep. We still have a long walk tomorrow before we reach the camp. We'll leave at first light."

"Okay," I said.

I leaned my head against the log and forced my eyes shut. Eventually, sleep found me and by the time I opened my eyes again, the sun was already up. I was lying with my head on Danny's shoulder, safely tucked under the crook of his arm. He was sound asleep, unaware of the sun's presence or of the last embers burning out. I tried to move without waking him, but the moment I shifted, his eyes opened.

There was an awkward moment between us, as we tried to untangle ourselves. We moved at the same time, standing up, and stepping in opposite directions. I brushed the dirt off my legs and clothes and noticed the red stains all down the front of them. Memories of the day before came flooding back to me all at once. I reached up to touch the right side of my face and felt immediate pain. My eye and lip were badly swollen and sore. I could only imagine the bruise that was spreading across them.

"Does it hurt?" Danny asked, cautiously moving closer to me.

"How bad does it look?" I turned sideways for him to see.

He touched the bruise gently with one of his fingers and I winced. He backed away quickly and said, "It looks worse than it is, but you'll be fine. You won't be entering any beauty pageants any time soon," he laughed.

I rolled my eyes and threw a small stick at him, which he easily avoided. He chose the direction we needed to go and started clearing a path calling out, "Come on 'Beauty Queen,' we've got a long way to go."

All the awkwardness of our morning faded as we fell into our normal routine of bickering. He led me deep into the jungle and, with no better choice, I followed him. Once, in the middle of one of our arguments—which he definitely started—he let a tree branch swing back and hit me. It wasn't a big branch, mostly leaves, but I wasn't paying attention. I was caught off balance, slipped, and fell backwards into the mud. Danny thought it was the funniest thing he'd ever seen, watching me roll around in the mud; so when he offered to help me up I pulled him down into the mud next to me. My clothes, already ruined from the blood, became covered in the wet mud and refused to dry for the rest of the day. By the time we started closing in on the rebel camp we were both in a frightful state.

"When we get to the camp, you need to stay close to me and do everything I say, understand?" He asked.

I was too tired to argue so I said, "Fine."

"I'm not joking, Mari. These men are extremely dangerous and volatile, if you offend them in any way we could end up in serious trouble. Just follow my lead." He paused. "And whatever you do, don't tell them who you are."

A few steps later, four men with AK-47s jumped out from every direction. They wore bandanas over their faces and were shouting things I couldn't understand. Danny kept his head down and raised his hands into the air.

"We are friends," he told them. "We are unarmed and we need help."

"Who are you?" The one in the red bandana shouted.

"We are friends," Danny said again. I followed his example, careful not to look any of them in the eye, with my hands high in the air.

One of them grabbed me from behind and patted me down looking for weapons. He found my knife and slid it into the waistband of his own cargo shorts. The third man searched Danny and uncovered a gun, hidden in the back waistband of his shorts, underneath his shirt.

"Where did you get a knife?" Danny asked me.

"Where did you get a gun?" I retorted.

"Quiet," the red bandana said; he was the one in charge. "You will come with us."

The men who searched us removed the bandanas from their faces and tied them over ours. My eyes and nearly my entire face was covered. I was completely blind. The bandana was wet and stunk of whatever it is that men stink of: sweat and dirt and perhaps a bit of blood. The man seized my upper arm roughly and pushed me the rest of the way to the camp. I tripped over things I couldn't see, but the man made sure I stayed upright. We walked a long way in the jungle down hidden paths, and crossed over a shallow river, which soaked through my sneakers. I heard voices ahead of us, and felt my feet reach the dry land. I could feel people staring at me, watching me being led like a criminal into their camp. A man shouted and others joined him, their voices too close for comfort.

"Danny?" One shouted above the rest.

"Kalu? Is that you?" Danny replied. "Tell these men to let us go."

"Remove this man's blindfold at once," the man named Kalu ordered. Danny's blindfold was taken off, but mine remained where it was. "This is the man who supplies our camp. What do you think you are doing?" Kalu asked the men.

Deep down I think I knew all along that Danny was aiding the rebels. All those "supply runs" with Jim's truck, the amount of meat in the truck the day we met, and even the way Danny spoke so animatedly when he was explaining the rebel's cause to me, were all clues pointing to the one truth that Danny was a rebel ally. Ken Saro-Wiwa and Jim said as much when they warned Danny about the path he was on. I should have picked up on it sooner. The Captain had been right; I knew more than I thought about the rebels.

"We did not recognize him," one of the rebels answered Kalu.

"And he was carrying this," another added.

"A gun? Why did you bring a gun here, Danny?" Kalu asked. "And why are you coming from the jungle and not the road."

"We ran into some trouble on the road," Danny replied. I need to speak with George."

"Come, I will take you to him."

Two pairs of footsteps moved away from me and I began to panic. "Danny, don't you dare leave me here like this!" I shouted at him.

"Who is the girl?" Kalu asked.

I heard Danny let out a sigh of annoyance, "She's alright. She's with me."

"Bring her then, but keep her blindfolded."

The man released his grip on my arm and I felt Danny's hand take its place.

"Why do I have to be blindfolded?" I whispered to him.

"Because they don't know if they can trust you yet, it's for George to decide," he whispered back.

"Who's George?"

"You'll see. Remember what I said, follow my lead."

"That's easy for you to say, you're not the one blindfolded." He pinched the soft part of my upper arm with his fingers and I cried, "Ow!"

"No arguing," he told me.

We travelled further into the rebel camp I couldn't see. When at last we stopped walking, I could feel a crowd forming around us. Kalu told us to wait where we were while he went to find the man called George. Even though we were standing still and I no longer needed help, Danny kept his hand around my arm protectively.

"Ah Danny, I have been expecting you," a new man's voice said.

Danny let go of my arm to shake hands with the man and I instantly felt his loss. Without Danny's hand I felt alone, facing an enemy that I couldn't see. I wanted to panic, but did my best not to show it.

"George, I'm so sorry I'm late my friend," Danny said. "As I told Kalu, we ran into some trouble on the road."

"Soldiers?"

"Soldiers and rebels." Danny added, "They were Northern rebels, I think."

"Will someone please take this blasted thing off my face?!" I interrupted them.

"You have brought a stranger into my camp Danny," George said. "Who is she?"

"She is from my village, and she has been kept blindfolded the whole time for your judgment," Danny reassured him.

"Can she be trusted?"

"She took a hit from the Captain, protecting an old man who had information about your camp."

I knew that old man knew something, I thought. "And I've got the bruises to prove it," I said. "Now can I take this thing off?"

The men in the camp laughed at me.

"You have spunk, girl. I like it," George said with humor in his voice. "Alright, you can take it off. Tell me your name."

I ripped the bandana off my face and at the same time said, "My name is Marienela."

When the bandana was completely removed I watched the man named George jump back in shock. The leader of the Outlaw's rebel camp seemed afraid of a seventeen year old girl. The rebel men stopped laughing, some of them raised and pointed their guns at me. Danny furrowed his brow in confusion over the way George and his men were behaving. The men were unsure what to do; it was up to me to say something.

"You must be Soboma George; the man from my mother's journal."

__Chapter 9__

"This is not possible," George spoke, mostly to himself.

"I get that a lot," I said.

George shook himself out of his shock and excitedly clapped his hands in front of him. "Kalu these two will be our guests for tonight. We shall have a celebration in Marienela's honor."

"Yes sir," Kalu replied.

"Please find them some accommodation for the night and take Marienela to a hut for some privacy." Turning his attention to me he said, "I imagine you will want to wash up."

"Yes please," I said suddenly aware of how dirty I felt.

"Find Marienela something to change into," he instructed Kalu. "Something befitting a rebel woman, I think you know what I am speaking of." Kalu nodded. George stepped forward and gently touched the bruised side of my face, "You are so much like your mother. I can see her defiance in your eyes. You have brought her back to me. Go and wash up, we have much to discuss."

Danny and I were separated and led to different sections of the camp. Kalu took me to a small hut and gave me a bucket of water to wash with. The water was cold, but felt good against my sore face. I washed my hands and face while I waited for Kalu to return with a change of clothes.

When he did he said, "I'm afraid we do not have women in the camp very often. George wanted me to give you this. He said it once belonged to your mother." I unraveled the cloth he was holding until it took the form of a dress, a very skimpy dress in a dark, almost burgundy, shade of red.

"I can't wear this out there, in front of all those men," I protested.

"I am sorry, it is all I can offer you. You cannot stay in your old clothes, they will need to be cleaned, but the blood will never wash out. I do not think you'll want to keep them."

"You're probably right," I agreed. I gave him a big, surrendering sigh and said, "Alright, I guess it's better than nothing."

"When you are ready come outside. I'll leave one of the men to escort you back to George and Danny."

"Where is Danny?" I asked out of curiosity.

"He is not far, you will see him as soon as you are dressed." He paused then added a warning, "You will not want to wander alone in the camp. We rarely have women here, it may not be safe for you, no matter who your mother was.

He left me again to change and finish washing up. I scrubbed my skin as clean as I could and stripped off my ruined clothing. Danny had my lighter and the rebels had taken away my knife. All that I had left was my passport. The dress Kalu gave me was extremely confusing. It took me forever to figure out how to wrap it around my body properly. The dress was a halter top that crisscrossed over my chest and then wrapped around my lower back and legs forming a skirt that barely reached the middle of my thigh. My entire back, arms, legs, and mid-section were bare; I might as well have been naked. I was completely exposed, on my own, in the middle of a camp of men with large guns and a desperate need for female companionship. My mother must have been braver than I thought, if she was willing to wear that dress in front of men like them. My only saving grace was that I was confident George would not let anything bad happen to Lila's daughter.

I found a safe way to store my passport in the folds of my skirt, which was not easy or comfortable, but I refused to leave it behind. My sneakers were damp from walking in the river so I decided to leave them off to let them dry and go barefoot through the camp. Being barefoot was not an uncommon thing in the village or in the camp, it wasn't ideal but it was only going to be for one night. Once I finished changing, I took a very deep breath and left the safety of the hut. Everyone's eyes found me all at once as I emerged. A young man, one of the youngest I'd seen so far in the camp, was standing guard outside my hut.

"I'm ready," I told him. "Are you the one who's taking me to George?"

He nodded, "Emmanuel Gladstone," he said offering me his hand. His grip was firm and his smile friendly. "Everyone calls me Tommy."

"Pleasure to meet you Tommy," I smiled.

He led me through the camp and I asked, "How long have you been in the camp, Tommy?"

"Only a couple of months, Miss," he answered politely

"Do you like being here?"

"It's okay, Miss. I am the youngest and newest member. Not many of the others like me yet."

"It sounds like you could use a friend," I said.

"Yes, Miss."

"Well Tommy, I could use a friend here too."

"You, Miss? What about the man you came with?"

"You can never have too many friends," I told him. "I'll tell you what, I'll be your friend if you'll be mine."

"Okay, Miss."

I stopped, "You can call me Mari."

I heeded Kalu's advice and stuck close to Tommy and the AK-47 he carried. I could feel the men's eyes on me everywhere I went. I observed my surroundings as Tommy cleared us a path back to George's hut. The rebels were a ragtag group of men ranging from young ones like Tommy to even a few older ones like the old man from the bus. They all dressed similarly in tattered shorts and tank tops and t-shirts, and every one of them carried a weapon carelessly at his side. There were guns and bullets everywhere I looked, and brass shell casings littered the ground. Many of the men possessed more than one weapon, owning both a gun, mostly AK-47s, and a machete. The machetes were scarier to me than the guns, all of them rusty and containing stains, for which I preferred not to know the origin. While I was changing inside the small hut, I was unaware of a commotion that had occurred among the men, the aftermath of which was still present. I asked Tommy if he knew what happened and he told me there had been some sort of fight, but he didn't know who was involved or why it started. Those things were common in the camp and didn't seem to worry Tommy or any of the others for that matter.

We arrived safely at George's hut where Kalu greeted us. "You can go in," he told me, "they're waiting for you."

He lifted the doorway curtain for me to pass under and followed me inside the small, rounded hut. George and Danny were sitting on old, plastic lawn chairs that had seen better days.

When Danny saw me in the dress he said, "Really Kalu, that's all you could find for her to wear?"

"We don't keep women's clothing in the camp," Kalu replied. "Besides, it is what George asked me to give her."

"She can't walk around like that in this camp," Danny told George.

"Come now Danny, I think she looks exquisite. Do you not think she looks beautiful?"

Danny squirmed uncomfortably in his chair, "That's not the point," he mumbled.

"Please Marienela," George said, "come and sit."

I obeyed, sitting down in the last empty chair. Kalu excused himself, leaving the three of us alone to talk. George was a slight man with a thin moustache and a presence that demanded obedience. No wonder he had become the leader of the rebels.

"We have much to talk about," George said, "but first I must know what happened on the road. Danny where are my supplies?"

"I hid the truck on the edge of the jungle. The soldiers shouldn't find it, but you need to send some of your men to retrieve it soon."

"I was right, you have been aiding the rebels," I interrupted.

"Danny plays a vital role for us," George said. "He brings us food and medical supplies, without him many of us would not survive. Tell me Danny, how many casualties were there at this road block?"

"We did not stay long enough to count. At least three soldiers and two rebels went down, but I don't know if they were injured or dead."

"And the old man from the bus," I added.

"He was definitely a rebel ally, I've seen him before," Danny said.

"He was shot trying to help me."

"I am sorry to hear that," George said, though I wasn't sure if he was sorry the old man died or sorry he lost one of his allies.

"I also shot the Captain," Danny said.

"You did?" George and I both asked at once.

Danny explained, "Mari was crawling towards the jungle and he saw her. He was running after her when I shot him." He paused then added, "He isn't dead. I only hurt him."

"You really did save my life then," I said. "Why didn't you tell me?"

"Would you have said thank you?"

"I doubt it."

"One of these days Mari, I'll get you to thank me," he teased and I rolled my eyes.

"I'm not sure that I like this abbreviation of your name very much," George thought out loud. "Mari does not have the same ring to it as Marienela. There is power in your name...if it is used properly."

"Why did my mother give me this name?" I asked him.

"It was me who told her what it meant."

"You? You're the one who named me?" Soboma George was an enemy to Ken Saro-Wiwa, a violent man, my mother's childhood friend, and the man who gave me my name.

"So it would seem," he replied.

"Where did you get it from?"

"I met a man in a bar in Port Harcourt when I was a teenager. He spoke several languages including Spanish. We discussed politics, the need for a rebellion, and the meaning of names. I told him only someone with a powerful name could lead people into an

213

uprising. He told me many different names and their meanings. Marienela was my favorite...Lila's too."

"Why Rebel Star?"

"Men use the stars in the sky to guide them, to help them find their way. A star that chooses to rebel can lead men in any direction it wants."

"You and my mother must have been very close," I said.

George nodded, "There was a short time when I believed we would spend the rest of our lives together, but plans always change."

"Did my father change your plans?"

"He was the beginning. I wanted to form my own group of rebels, Lila was helping me, and then *he* came along. He fell in love the moment he set eyes on her and proposed not long after. He led a team of surveyors who were testing Ogoniland for oil and we knew he would quickly rise into a position of power at the oil company. We came up with a new plan. Lila would return to London with him and discover his plans for the land. She would try to sabotage the company from within using her new husband's money and position. If she could bring the company down from London, then there would be no need for our rebel group here. Then she was supposed to come home to me."

"You sent my mother to be a spy for you?"

"It was her decision."

"What happened next?"

"You and your brother. You were not a part of the plan. Lila was unable to discover any secret information from the company. She was ready to leave and sent me word to be prepared to pick her and her children up from the airport a week later. She never arrived and I never heard from her again. About a year later, your father showed up in the village bearing Lila's ashes. He told Naomi that she died of an illness, then took her ashes to Agbokim Falls. No one went with him and the rest of us were forced to move on with nothing but her memory."

"You describe her as a rebel and a spy, you make her sound strong, but she wasn't strong. She was weak. She wasn't even strong enough to fight off a cold. She got sick and never got better," hearing such things about my mother's past made me mad at her for leaving us.

"Lila was *not* weak. You are a fool if you think that." He paused. "She was strong, a fighter, and I believe that you are too."

"I'm not strong," I said ashamed.

"Stronger than you think," Danny said quietly, under his breath. I was so involved in my conversation with George that I hardly remembered Danny was there.

I didn't have a chance to respond to his comment because George quickly stood up and said excitedly, "Let me show you around my camp." He offered me a hand to help me up from the chair and we exited the hut. Outside, Tommy and Kalu were waiting.

"Tommy, you may leave us now, you are on guard duty for tonight," George instructed him.

"Yes sir," Tommy said and left us.

"Kalu, have you prepared a place for Danny and Marienela to sleep for tonight?"

"Yes sir. Tommy convinced the others to leave the smaller hut empty for them to share tonight."

"Share?" I interrupted.

"Mari, I have to talk to you," Danny said in a hushed voice only I could hear. "Now."

I ignored him, "Danny and I are sharing a hut tonight?"

"Space is limited in the camp, besides Danny told us you are a couple. I hardly think you would mind sharing a bed."

"Danny said what?" I asked through clenched teeth.

"Yeah about that, we really need to talk," Danny said again. "George do you mind if we have a minute alone?"

"Of course," George replied.

Danny pulled me back inside the hut where no one would hear us. "I'm sorry, I haven't had a chance to explain."

"You better explain now because I'm two seconds from putting my fist in your face."

"I was taken to change and get cleaned up like you and when I was coming back to meet you and George I overheard a couple of the men talking about you. They said...well it wasn't good."

"So you told everyone you were my boyfriend?"

"No. I punched one of them."

"You what?"

"I got into a fight with both of them, then Kalu pulled us apart."

"I'm still waiting for the part where we became a couple," I said crossing my arms over my chest.

"It's hard to explain, but Kalu asked what we were fighting over and apparently unless a woman is spoken for, then getting into a fight over her is a big 'no-no,' so I told him you *were* spoken for." He finished. "They will be testing us now, to see if I was lying."

"I thought these people were your friends, why would Kalu be testing you?"

"Make no mistake Mari, there are no friends amongst the rebels. They are men who like the sight of blood and defy any sign of authority other than their leader. Some of them are friendly enough, but none of them are good men."

"But you feed them."

Danny nodded, "That's an entirely different matter. For now, I just need you to pretend. One night and then we're out of here and we can go back to hating each other. Can you do that?"

"Do I have a choice?"

"Not really, no."

"Then yes."

George led us around the camp, the men stepping aside respectfully as we walked by, staring at us curiously and eyeing me in my dress. There were only a few huts in the camp, most of the men slept either in tents or outside by the fires. In the rainy seasons they crammed into the huts and tents, but an unfortunate few would be forced to remain outside. A large bonfire was situated in the middle of the camp directly across from George's hut. The men often gathered there to eat, be given instructions from George, and even to pray. On the same day we arrived in the camp, a priest from a nearby village, a rebel supporter, was also visiting. Many of the men were Catholic and the priest, known only as Father, visited regularly to pray over the men and to accept their confessions.

The priest saw us and approached. He told George, "I must be going soon."

George clapped his hand on the priest's back and said, "Please, come and meet my friends, Father. This is Danny and Marienela."

We each shook the priest's hand. "Pleasure to meet you both," he said.

"You must stay and eat with us tonight," George said. "We are having a celebration in honor of my two friends here."

"Thank you for your kind offer, but..."

"I won't take no for an answer," George cut him off.

"Well then, it seems you leave me no choice. I would be happy to stay and celebrate with you," the priest replied.

George smiled and shouted an order to the men nearest him to find a place for the priest to sleep. The priest left us and we continued our tour. I played my part of Danny's fake girlfriend well, holding his hand and pretending like we were a happy couple. I saw that Danny was right; if we were caught in our lie or if the men knew I was available, things would not go well for either of us.

At dusk, when the sun was setting, our tour ended and the bonfire was lit. Tommy set up an old lawn chair for me between Danny and George. The others sat in a large, rather messy, circle around the fire. I asked Tommy if he would like to sit with me, but he declined. He had already eaten his small portion of the food and would be on guard duty for the rest of the night, preventing him from joining the celebrations.

Danny leaned over to me and said, "When you're handed something, always pass to the right, never the left."

"Why?" I asked.

"The left hand is considered dirty, so it's rude to offer anything to the left."

I was given a stick with several large hunks of meat on it and told I could start eating. I slid a piece of the meat off and popped it into my mouth. It had been barbequed over the fire and coated with spices that burned my tongue.

223

"It's called *Suya*," Danny told me.

"What kind of meat is it?" I knew it wasn't beef or chicken.

"Goat," he said.

Surprisingly I didn't mind the goat meat. It was actually quite delicious. I was allowed to eat the entire stick of meat by myself, but everything else had to be shared. A can filled with an orange, pasty substance was handed to me by George. I was required to dip my fingers into the can and take whatever food stuck to them. I passed the can using my right hand, which was covered in food, to Danny who was on my right. George gave me an approving nod recognizing I knew the proper traditions of his culture. Before I licked the orange goo off my fingers I inspected it.

"Mashed yams," Danny said before I could ask.

Knowing yams were a common vegetable, I gave them a try. I cleaned off every bit of the yams from my fingers and next accepted a can of black beans. I dipped my fingers into the beans and passed the can to Danny. We continued to eat that way until everyone had their fair share of the food. George handed me a large gourd of white liquid and told me to drink.

"What is it?" I asked.

"*Ogogoro*," he answered.

"Palm wine," Danny interpreted for me.

I became aware that all of the rebels were watching me. I lifted the gourd to my mouth and took a small mouthful. The tart liquid burned all the way down my throat and into my stomach, bringing tears to my eyes. I coughed and the men laughed. They were still watching me expectantly, so I stood up and took a much bigger gulp for all of them to see. The burn wasn't as bad the second time and the men cheered excitedly for me.

"I'll take that," Danny said plucking the gourd from my hands. "This stuff is dangerous, you should probably stay away from it."

Several gourds of palm wine were passed around for the rest of the night. I made sure every time a gourd was handed to me that Danny could see me take a large swig. I took his warning as a challenge and a couple of hours later I was regretting it. A warmth spread through my body and my head began to feel fuzzy. I've been drunk before,--I was a rich teenage girl, with a boring life, what else was I going to do for fun?— but the palm wine's effect was stronger than average alcohol. Kalu informed me that palm wine wasn't really a wine at all. It was made from the sap of palm trees and then distilled until it turned into a liquor that was stronger than gin.

I stayed in my chair for most of the night watching the men get drunk and then laugh and sing and dance around the fire. George was busy talking to the priest next to him and Danny left me alone to join some of the others. Kalu took his seat, but ignored me.

After a while, I asked Kalu, "Where is Danny?" He was no longer within my sight and I grew nervous at being alone with all the rebels.

Kalu was too busy having a drunken conversation with his men to bother with me, so he simply pointed across the fire where I spotted Danny. He was drinking and laughing with some of the others; he was in his element, enjoying himself, and I was more than a little jealous. I left my chair and moved closer to the fire. The night was chilly, so I put my hands closer to the flames to warm them. Someone gave me the palm wine again and I drank deeply from the gourd. I handed it off to another man and used the back of my hand to wipe my mouth. When I looked up, Danny's eyes met mine over the flames. The first time we saw each other was from across a fire. He watched me and I watched him. Then he tilted his head, inviting me to join him.

A Rebel Star

That's the last thing I remember.

★♦★

My head ached. I opened my eyes but the light burned them. *Why did I drink all that palm wine?* I asked myself. *Okay,* I thought, *just open your eyes.* I forced them open and immediately regretted it. I found myself lying on a straw mattress, like the one I slept on in Naomi's home. I found myself lying with my head on Danny's chest. *Not again,* I thought. I moved away from him and he shifted. He opened his eyes and moaned in pain.

"That's what you get for drinking so much last night," I scolded myself and him at the same time.

"Look who's talking," he retorted crankily. "What time is it?"

"Do I look like I'm wearing a watch?"

A Rebel Star

I noticed that I was in fact wearing something on my wrist, but it wasn't a watch. I was wearing a beautiful bracelet made up of three rows of white shells on a stretchy string that fitted itself to my wrist. I ran my fingers around the bracelet, wondering where it came from. I wasn't paying attention, so when Danny grabbed my arm it made me jump.

"Where did you get this?" He asked. His fingers squeezed around my arm leaving a mark.

"I don't know," I told him.

"Who gave this to you?" He was almost shouting.

"I don't remember," I shouted back. "Let go of me your hurting my arm."

He dropped my arm and stood up quickly. He seemed tired from the long night and more than a little frustrated. He peeked beyond the doorway curtain to the camp outside and said, "Do me a favor and wait here. I'm going to find out when they're going to get the truck. Do *not* leave this hut."

"Fine," I said.

He left me alone and I plopped back down on the straw bed, closing my eyes. I fell asleep while I waited for him to return, only rousing when I heard the curtain lifting. I yawned and sat up, leaning my back against the mud wall, and tried to rub the sleep from my eyes.

"Well?" I asked Danny.

"Get up quickly and get your stuff," he ordered me with a worried look on his face.

"Why the rush? Is the truck here already?"

"We need to leave now."

Chapter 10

"What's wrong?" I asked.

"The truck is here, we need to move fast. All the men are gathered around the fire. Something's happening and we need to be out of here before it does."

"How bad do you think it is?"

"These men don't usually wake up early after a night of drinking. Most days they sleep 'til late afternoon. When I went outside, all of them were already up, I don't even want to find out why." I slipped my feet into my damp sneakers and gathered up my clothes. "We need to keep moving, don't stop for anything or anyone."

Danny's plan would have worked if only Kalu hadn't walked into our hut the second the words were out of Danny's mouth.

"George wishes to see you both before you leave," he told us.

"We really need to get back home," Danny protested.

"It will not take long, he only wants to say goodbye to the girl."

He ducked below the door curtain leaving us little choice but to follow him. Danny reached over and took my hand continuing our pretense of being a couple. "Let's do this as quickly as possible."

He pulled me behind him, practically dragging me through the camp. The men were tired. They shuffled into their meeting place with their machetes on their hips, guns in hand, and bitter looks written on their faces. I imagined their heads pounding as badly as mine and wondered if any of them were regretting the amount of palm wine they drank. They appeared more than tired; they seemed angry. No, they seemed dangerous.

George was delighted to see us when we reached him. He shook Danny's hand and kissed me on both cheeks, "You look beautiful this morning, my dear."

Danny spoke before I could, "We wanted to thank you for your hospitality last night, it was greatly appreciated, but I think it is time for us to go."

One of the rebels walked by us and I recognized him as one of the men who had brought Danny and me into the camp. Sticking out of the waistband of his khaki shorts was my mother's knife which he had taken from me in the jungle. "Hey," I called out to him. He stopped in his tracks. "That knife is mine, I want it back." The man, unused to returning items he nicked from others, looked to George who gestured for him to give me the knife. The man took it out of his shorts and handed it over to me. I thanked him and slid the knife into the top of my skirt, in the front where everyone could see it.

George laughed, "You have a fire inside you girl. A rebel fire. Are you sure you want to leave so soon?" He asked Danny. "I hate to lose the company of this amazing creature," he looked at me and I could feel my cheeks turning red.

"We really need to get home, our families will start to worry about us," Danny replied, his voice uneasy.

George thought for a moment, then declared, "It is too early for you to leave, I insist that you stay a while longer and eat with us one more time."

A Rebel Star

"How can we refuse such a generous offer? We will be happy to stay for the morning, but we will have to leave you this afternoon."

"Very well," George clapped his hands together, "but first we have some business matters to attend to." To his men he shouted, "Bring him forward!"

Two of the rebels pushed through the others, dragging a person between them. It was Tommy. They threw him down on the ground at George's feet and stepped back. Tommy remained on his knees with his head facing the ground in fear.

"What's going on?" I whispered to Danny.

"I don't know," he answered, "but whatever happens keep quiet and don't interfere." Danny moved so that he was directly in front of me as if shielding me from what was to come.

George said in a loud voice, "This man has been caught sleeping at his post. This is a crime against us all,

235

for it threatens the safety of this camp and each one of us. Therefore, it is a crime deserving of punishment. Do you have anything you wish to say?" He asked Tommy.

"I'm so sorry, I did not mean to, please forgive me," Tommy pleaded.

"Sorry is not good enough. Would 'sorry' have saved us from a soldier's attack? Would it have given us fair warning so that we could prepare to defend ourselves? Your 'sorry' is no good here."

Tommy's eyes filled with tears. He knew there was no way out of whatever punishment George chose to give him. He tilted his head down in shame and awaited George's judgment.

"You are young and have not been with us long, but that will not save you from punishment. You must be taught a lesson so that you will not fail us again. Do you understand?"

"Yes sir," Tommy answered in a weak voice.

"You are to receive 18 lashes, to be given to you by the men you failed to protect. Who will be first?" He asked his men.

One of the biggest men in the camp stepped forward. He approached and handed Kalu his gun. In exchange Kalu gave the man a stick with several pieces of long rope hanging off one end. Each rope had two or three knots tied at different intervals. I knew what would happen next and I knew I couldn't watch. I shifted forward a bit and Danny stopped me. He laced his fingers through mine and moved so that I was almost completely behind him. He wasn't protecting me from the men, he was protecting me from myself. He must have known exactly what George's orders would be and he knew how I would react.

Tommy was forced to lie on the ground on his stomach and remove his shirt, leaving his bare back exposed. The man raised the whip high in the air and brought it crashing down on Tommy's back. The ropes cracked against his flesh leaving red lines in their wake.

Danny squeezed my hand. A second man volunteered and repeated the act. I shut my eyes, but I could not escape the sound of the whip cracking, or of Tommy's screams. The second man handed the whip to a third, who raised it above his head.

"Stop!" I screamed. The man did not listen and the whip hit Tommy's back for a third time. I ran to Tommy's side, nearly knocking Danny over, and yelled, "Stop!" again as the whip was given to a fourth man.

"Mari!" Danny yelled. "Get away from there!"

The fourth man ignored us, raised the whip, and brought it down. I threw myself over Tommy, under the path of the whip, and felt it snap across the top of my back and shoulders. Danny, enraged, launched himself at the man holding the whip and knocked him to the ground. The man jumped up and punched Danny in the face. The rebels cheered and exchanged bets on Danny and the man. Tommy's punishment was forgotten, but Danny's was just beginning.

The fight lasted too long. Danny was tough, but his opponent was twice his size. Tommy, still lying on the ground, was moaning with pain. My own back stung from the bite of the whip, but I ignored the ache. Danny's involvement was my fault, I needed to stop the fight. George was sitting in his chair watching them as if it were all a game. I left poor Tommy lying on the ground and stood up in front of George, blocking his view of the fight.

"Make this stop," I ordered him.

"You interrupted a punishment. This is the consequence," he said nonchalantly.

"You have to end this. It was my fault, not Danny's. Punish me instead."

"If you tempt me again, I *will* accept your offer," he threatened and I believed him. Being Lila's daughter only had so many advantages; there was one more thing I could try.

I got down on my knees in front of him, "I am begging you, please end this." He studied me from his seat, saying nothing. I added, "In honor of my mother's memory."

George stared deeply into my pleading eyes. Behind me I could hear the sounds of Danny's fight and Tommy's sobs of pain. My heart pounded in my chest, but I showed no fear. George's attitude and demeanor changed. He smiled at me and motioned for Kalu to put an end to the fight. Danny was pulled away from the rebel and returned to me. His lip was bloody and several bruises were appearing on his face and body, but he was mostly unharmed. It was over. We were safe.

"You're tougher than you look," I teased.

"You should see me when I'm not hung over," he grinned.

George was not offended by our actions, he was instead impressed with our bravery. "Your mother was brave, but she never would have defied me the way you did. You have shown you deserve your name. We could use more fighters like the two of you. Perhaps you would like to stay."

"Thank you for such a generous offer," Danny said, "but I'm afraid we have to decline."

"Very well," George said, more than a little disappointed.

A few of the men helped Tommy to his feet and led him away to have his back taken care of. When he walked by us he stopped and took my hand. "You are a good friend," he told me.

George, agreeing that it was a good time for us to leave, walked with us to the truck. I asked him, "What will happen to Tommy now?"

He merely shrugged his shoulders, "His back will be cleaned and he will rejoin the men. He's had his punishment for now. I do not believe he will be making the same mistake again."

"So he's safe?"

"You have rescued him from further punishment if that's what you mean."

George stopped me before we reached the truck and slipped a small piece of folded paper into my hand. "Take this and memorize it," he told me.

I unfolded the paper until I could see that there was a phone number written in the middle. A Port Harcourt number, and nothing else.

"It is the number for a bar in Port Harcourt, the one where I learned your name. The owner is a friend of mine, a rebel supporter. This is how you can reach me if you are ever in need of anything. The owner will give you a time to call back and I will answer when you do. You will always be welcome in this camp, Marienela."

He walked away without saying goodbye.

"You're awfully quiet for once," Danny said. We were close to the main road, near where the road block originally stopped my bus. George's men recovered the truck early in the morning—I don't know how after all the palm wine they drank—and checked to make sure the road was clear enough for us to leave. The soldiers and all the bodies were cleaned up as if nothing had ever happened. Once we got back to that spot Danny could turn south and take us back to our village.

"Do they always whip men for falling asleep at their post?"

Danny shook his head, "Sometimes they kill them. It's what they call Jungle Justice." He looked over at me, "Are you alright?"

"I'm fine," I replied in a low voice.

"What did George say to you before we left?"

"He gave me a way to get in contact with him if I ever need his help."

"Let's hope that never happens."

I sat quietly, staring out the window, thinking about everything that happened to us. A thought was turning in the back of my mind and refused to go away. "Ken Saro-Wiwa told me you would lead me to the man who gave me my name, is that why you decided to take me into the camp?"

"No."

"Then why? Why did you bring me there if it was so dangerous? We could've hid in the jungle for one more night then went back to get the truck ourselves. Or we could've followed the river back to the village. It would have taken longer, but how much worse would it have been?"

Danny sighed in frustration, "How long do you think you would have lasted in the jungle without food or shelter? The camp wasn't far, we were fed and given a roof over our heads."

He was holding something back from me, I could sense it, "Let me ask you a different question: if you hadn't followed me and my bus hadn't been stopped at that road block, would you have found another way to bring me into the camp?"

Danny said nothing.

"It took us nearly a whole day, in the opposite direction of the village, to get there. We could have easily spent that time going south towards home. Instead, you told me you had a plan and then dragged me through the jungle into a rebel camp full of dangerous men. What *was* your plan? Did you think George would realize who I was and instead of welcoming me, were you hoping he would ransom me off to my father?"

Danny still said nothing.

"You saw an opportunity to get rid of me and make a little profit, so you took it, only it backfired when you realized George would never betray my mother's memory like that. You changed your mind about the whole thing and then saw that you might be in danger if George found out the truth. You pretended to be my boyfriend to save your own skin. I'm right aren't I?"

I gave him a few seconds to answer, but he didn't say a word.

"Stop the truck," I ordered him. He ignored me, and kept his foot firmly pressed against the gas pedal. I opened my door while the truck was still moving, and prepared to jump out.

"What are you doing?!" Danny shouted as he slammed the truck's brakes. As soon as it stopped moving, I got out and started walking down the road. "Get back in the truck Mari," Danny yelled.

"I'm not going anywhere with you."

I kept walking and he drove the truck alongside me, talking to me through his open window, "What are you going to do then, walk back? You'll never make it on foot with no water. You'll die of dehydration before you're even halfway."

"Not if I go into the jungle and follow the river back."

"That's not a terrible idea, except for the thousands of poisonous bugs, snakes, and plants you don't know how to identify, and I still have your lighter so there's no way for you to start a fire at night to keep the big animals away."

"I'll make it."

"Maybe, maybe not." He stopped the truck beside me, "Or you can get into the truck and come with me."

"Why, so you can take me to another rebel camp and see if they're willing to ransom me off?"

"Will you give me a chance to explain myself?"

I stopped walking, "Sure, explain yourself."

Danny shook his head, "Not here, the road may not be safe."

I stepped away and started walking again.

"Oh for crying out loud, Mari. Please get into the truck," he begged. "I'll explain once we get to where we're going."

Saying nothing more, I climbed into the passenger seat. Danny turned the truck to the North, the opposite direction from the village.

"Where are we going?" I asked grumpily.

Danny faced me with a wide grin, "You'll see."

I refused to talk to him for the rest of the ride. My eyes grew heavy and the rocking of the truck lulled me into a dreamless sleep. We weren't stopped at anymore road blocks, and our ride was smooth and uneventful as we made our way to Danny's surprise destination. A few hours after falling asleep, he gently nudged me awake.

"Time to wake up," he told me.

I felt groggy and stiff, "Where are we?"

Danny motioned for me to look out the window where there was a small path cut between the jungle trees awaiting us. "We have a bit of a walk ahead of us, but we're almost there."

"Not the jungle again," I whined, throwing my head back against the seat.

"Yup. Come on, we need to get moving if we want to get there before dark."

I rubbed my eyes and yawned, "How far do we have to go?"

"You'll see," was all he would say.

Danny got out and I reluctantly followed. There was a single back pack in the bed of the truck. Danny secured the bag over his shoulders and I asked him what was in it. He grunted, "Supplies," then locked the truck and started down the trail.

The thin trail twisted and turned through the rough jungle. Giant roots and rocks poked up out of the dirt at the most random intervals and every time I looked down to avoid tripping over one I would walk straight into a tree branch. Danny slowed his pace in order for me to keep up. I tried my best not to complain, but the hike was killing me. My calves burned, my feet hurt, and the mosquitoes, who mercilessly bit every inch of my bare skin, were out in droves. I was miserable.

There was a point where the trail forked: one section continued straight and flat in front of us, and the second gradually rose up a large, mountain-like hill that we would have to climb. Danny stopped and pulled a canteen out from his bag. "Here," he handed it to me first. The water tasted fresh though not very cool and I drank deeply from it, then handed it back so Danny could drink too. When we finished taking turns, Danny put the canteen back into his bag and put the bag back on his shoulders.

"Please tell me we're taking the nice easy trail ahead of us," I pleaded.

Danny smiled mischievously, "Nope."

"Of course we're not."

"Don't worry, you'll thank me for it later."

"I seriously doubt that."

"Let's go, we only have a couple hours left 'til dark."

"I swear I'm going to kill you if we don't get to wherever we're going soon," I muttered.

He laughed and led the way up the slope. The first few meters were like walking up a steep hill, but as we neared the top we began to use our hands and feet to climb. Large rocks jutted out from the dirt, covered in vines and roots. We took our time finding safe, strong foot and hand holds, inching further and further up. The climb was both exhausting and exhilarating. I paused to rest in a safe spot and could hear the jungle birds chatting away, high in the trees, and in the distance there was the sound of water. A lot of water. Danny was at the crest of our mountain, pulling himself up and over the top. *Not much further,* I told myself. I reached up for the next hold, a large, thick vine, and felt it pull away from the rock face. I caught myself on my original hold, keeping my balance with my other hand and my feet, but the vine was ripped clean away from the rock. I was only a couple feet from the top, but I was stuck with no more holds for my hand. I felt along the rock's bumpy surface, but there was nothing for me to grip. Foolishly, I glanced over my shoulder for a glimpse of the ground below and felt my stomach turn in fear. It was a long way down, and I was stuck.

"Need a little help?" Danny asked from above.

I looked up and saw him leaning over the edge smiling and offering me his hand. I didn't hesitate. I reached up and took hold of his arm. He pulled me the rest of the way up until I was kneeling at his feet on the top. Danny helped me to my feet and I brushed the dirt of my hands and knees and fought to catch my breath.

"I think it's time for that thank you," Danny said grinning, but he wasn't talking about helping me up. He lifted a giant, green leaf out of the way to clear my view.

My breath caught in my throat. I lost all words. I had never seen anything so brilliant, so spectacular.

"Welcome to Agbokim Falls," Danny said.

Chapter 11

My mother's words came nowhere near to capturing the brilliance of Agbokim Falls; there were no words capable for such a description. The roar of the water was deafening. The vibrancy of the green foliage was blinding. The white water crashed over the cliff top in seven perfect curtains and plunged into the pool below sending up a large spray upon impact. The thick moisture in the air surrounding us soaked into my skin and clothing giving me goose bumps. The air blowing from the water was a cool contrast to the jungle's humidity. Danny and I stood in awe of the falls' magnificence.

In my mind I imagined the place we were standing to be the same place my mother sat when she visited the falls. I tried to picture my father climbing up the cliff, carrying her urn, and spreading her ashes once he reached the top. I closed my eyes and I swore I could feel my mother's presence all around me. I was so entranced by the beauty of the falls that I almost forgot Danny was there. He unzipped his bag and pulled out a folded tarp, then gathered up a few sticks and a small rock. He secured the tarp to a thick tree branch and I held the bottom in place as he used the rock to drive the sticks through the tarp and into the ground. He tested the tarp by giving it a hard tug, making sure it wouldn't fall on us as we slept. We gathered enough firewood to last the night and cooked a can of beans over the flames. We ate like the rebels, taking turns with the can until the food was gone. The sky was pink and orange, and reflected in the water. When it became dark, black really, we made ourselves comfortable under the tarp and fell asleep to the sound of the falls.

Thoughts of my mother haunted my dreams. I saw her writing in her journal perched on the edge of the cliff, and swimming in the river below. I saw Father tearlessly releasing her ashes into the breeze that blew off the water; the grey dust of her remains dancing in the mist and down the river. I pictured her happy for the first time in a long time.

I woke up alone in our make-shift shelter and found Danny sitting near the edge, admiring the view. I said, "Good morning," and sat down beside him.

"I think we should move our camp to the bottom. I only brought us up here for the view, but it's not really practical to stay here. I say we climb down and follow the other trail for a better place to set up."

"How long are we staying?" I asked.

"I was thinking we would stay one more night then head back, what do you think?"

I nodded in agreement.

We were in no rush. We spent the majority of our morning relaxing on the cliff top, taking in the falls before we packed up and began our trip down. Climbing down was a lot more difficult than climbing up. Danny went first—I warned him he better not be staring up my dress which made him laugh—and coached me from below on where the best holds were and which dangerous roots to avoid. I missed the last foot hold and Danny had to catch me before I fell. He caught me around my waist, his hands gripping the bare skin above the top of my skirt. I straightened up and he removed his hands; I could still feel the warmth of them long after they were gone.

The second trail was much quicker and easier to navigate. We followed it all the way to the large pool below the falls and found a dry place to set up the tarp.

The heat was relentless, so we put our things down and followed the water downstream, where the current was weak enough for us to wade in. I eased into the cool water with my dress still on. The marks on my back that the whip left behind stung forcing me to stand up quickly. Danny stripped his shirt off giving me my first glimpse of his bruises from his fights with the rebels. The side of his stomach was a deep purple rimmed in light green.

"Are you alright?" I asked him.

He seemed to have forgotten about me. He looked up and grinned. "I've had worse." He flinched a little as he moved. "How is your back?"

"It stings a little."

"Let me see."

I returned to the river bank beside him and turned my back for him to see. He ran his fingers gently over the thin, raised lines. "Your skin didn't break. You'll be fine in a few days, just a bit sore."

"How about you?"

"I'll be fine, nothing but a few bruises."

I asked a question that was burning in the back of my mind. "How did you know?"

"Know what?"

"That I would try to stop Tommy's punishment."

"Because you did the same for my brother in the market, and for the old man at the road block. You seem to be in the habit of putting yourself in between people and danger."

We washed ourselves in the refreshing water and swam for what felt like hours. Time slowed as we lay out on the rocks and let the sun dry us. I laid on my stomach—my back was too sore to lay against the rough rocks. I rested my head on my arms, and quietly dozed off. Danny was beside me on his back, his eyes closed. I lifted my head up and watched him. He opened one eye and grunted.

"I'm waiting," I said.

"For..."

"Your explanation."

He sighed, "Right now?"

"It's as good a time as any."

Reluctantly he sat up, "Look it's not what you're thinking."

"Why did you bring me to the rebel camp?"

"I was on my way with the food and supplies, and I was already delayed by following you. When I ditched the truck to help you, I knew I still needed to get to the camp. George gives me the money to pay for the supplies, if I didn't show up he would have thought I was stealing from him. You've seen what he's capable of, I kept thinking the whole way how I could stay in his good favor and I realized the answer was right there in front of me all along: you. The supplies might be late or even lost, but I was bringing him the daughter of his worst enemy. I figured he might ransom you off for a lot of money; you would go back home, and I wouldn't be in any trouble."

"You were willing to trade my life for yours? What if he hadn't decided to keep me a hostage? He could have killed me right there on the spot for revenge and it would have been your fault!"

Danny shook his head, "You're worth more to him alive than dead. I knew he wouldn't kill you, but when George learned who you were everything changed. I had no idea Ken Saro-Wiwa was talking about George when we met him on "Ogoni Day." The truth turned out to be my better option. I abandoned his supplies to save the life of the daughter of the woman he loved. He called me into his hut and I told him everything that happened."

261

"And pretending to be my boyfriend? How did that fit into your story?"

"That part was an accident. I felt guilty about my plans to give you to the rebels, so when I heard a couple of the men talking about you I really did get into a fight with them. I brought you there, it was my responsibility to get you back out safely."

"And you brought me here afterwards…"

"To apologize." He grinned, "So, will you forgive me?"

"I'm still deciding."

We returned to our new campsite to set up for the night. Collecting firewood alone gave me the time and space I needed to think about everything Danny told me. I mulled over everything he said and in the end decided, much to my own surprise, that I wasn't angry with him. How could I judge someone else for being selfish? I realized that if our roles were reversed I would have done the exact same thing without even thinking twice about it.

Night closed in around us and Danny showed me the proper way to build and light a fire. We used the smaller sticks to form a tee-pee shape around a bundle of leaves and things that would catch a flame quickly, called kindling. As the small flames grew, we added larger and larger sticks until the fire was big enough to last most of the night. I noticed Danny eyeing my wrist where I was still wearing the white shell bracelet someone had given me in the rebel camp.

"This belongs to you, doesn't it?" I asked him and he nodded in reply. "Why did you give it to me?"

"I don't remember," he shook his head while shifting the sticks on the fire. He was acting strangely, and I noticed for the first time a wide section of pale skin around his wrist in the shape of the bracelet.

"It's important to you, isn't it?" Again he only nodded. "Who was she?"

"Who?" He finally looked at me.

"The girl who owned this bracelet."

Expecting some grand tale of an old romance I was surprised when Danny answered, "She was my sister." I didn't want to push him, but my thoughts urged him on. A few moments later he continued, "She was a year older than me and we were very close. We did everything together. She was crazy over our little brother, always insisting we bring him with us everywhere we went. She wanted to become a school teacher, to help build the first school here in our village for the children in Ogoniland." He smiled at the memory. "I made her that bracelet when I was young, she never took it off, not until..."

When he didn't say anything more I asked, "What happened to her?"

His face darkened, "She was killed by a government soldier. They come into the villages whenever they want, questioning people about the rebels, just like what they did to you at the road block. It's all for show though, the real reason they come is because they want to drive us off the land. Your father's company pays the soldiers and the soldiers attack the villages. They came one day and I wasn't there. They set fire to some of the huts and a few of the villagers fought back. Naomi's husband, my sister, Natalie's father, all of them were shot down on the orders of one man."

"The captain."

He nodded, "The captain. I took that bracelet off my sister's arm before we buried her and vowed I would avenge her death. I've worn it every day since to remind myself why I've sided with the rebels and their cause."

I waited for him to say more; I slipped the bracelet off my wrist and handed it back to him. "You said you shot the captain to save me...I hope you killed him."

"I was too far away, I think I only wounded him."
He slid the bracelet back into its place on his wrist.

"Then you'll finish him off next time."

After a while of silently watching the flames consume the wood, Danny asked, "Why did you come to Nigeria?"

"My father gave me a choice. I could go to University to learn a trade or skill that would make me miserable for the rest of my life, work for him at the oil company, or marry a man I didn't love so that our two families could combine their money."

"So you ran away."

"I found a journal my mother wrote for me and my brother. She said she always wanted us to see her home, so I packed a bag and bought a plane ticket."

He asked more questions about my life in London and I told him everything. He listened to my stories intently, laughing in all the right places and rolling his eyes at my foolish friend Kirstin. We talked until we fell asleep under the cover of our tarp, with millions of stars beaming above us.

Chapter 12

"Can I drive?'

We were standing next to the truck, early in the morning, preparing to leave the waterfalls behind and start our journey home.

"Do you know how?" Danny asked, his eyebrows raised in surprise.

"Of course!" I lied.

When I was sixteen—a whole year before I went to live in Nigeria—I had a sudden urge to learn how to drive, and persuaded our chauffer to teach me. After three lessons and a fender bender, he gave up, calling me hopeless. In London there was never a need for me to know how to drive, a taxi or our driver was always on hand to pick me up and take me where I wanted to go. In Nigeria, who knew what skills I would need to get by? Watching Danny constantly driving the truck renewed my desire to learn.

"Okay then," he tossed me the keys and I hopped into the driver's seat giddy with excitement. I turned the key and the engine coughed, but did not start. I tried a second time with the same result.

"Mari…"

"Give me a sec," I turned the key again, but nothing happened.

"You have to use the clutch," Danny said.

"I know that!" I looked down on the floor and saw three different pedals. "Now which one is the clutch?" I muttered to myself.

Danny laughed, "You liar. You've never driven a day in your life have you?"

"Yes I have. Our driver gave me a few lessons, but he gave up when I smashed the front of his car."

Danny shook his head, but he was smiling. Instead of being angry or annoyed with me he said, "The clutch is the one on the far left. Push it down all the way to the floor and then turn the key."

I followed his instructions and the engine purred to life. Danny gave me a quick lesson on how and when to switch gears and, after a few practice attempts, we were successfully on our way back to the village. As soon as we reached the main, dirt road our ride was fairly smooth. Danny let me drive fast to practice shifting into the higher gears. Driving a manual truck was much more complicated than driving an automatic like the one we owned in London, but on the flat, open Nigerian roads I had plenty of space to learn. Danny was extremely patient with me, even though there were many times when I was sure he was going to make me pull over and switch places with him. He never did. In a matter of hours I had almost completely mastered the art of driving and Danny trusted me enough to close his eyes and take a nap. By late afternoon we were only three hours away from the village and I was getting tired, but Danny was sound asleep and I didn't have the heart to wake him up. In that moment, while Danny slept and I was truly alone, I finally felt the freedom I was searching for. I was completely in charge of my own life, with no one to answer to, no rules to follow, and no plans for the future. I was free!

A car approached from the other direction, one of the very few I had seen all day. I slowed down as it drove by and the man in the front seat waved to me, only it was not a friendly wave, it was a wave of warning. I slowed the truck a little more and squinted my eyes hoping to see further down the road. There were small, dark figures, like people, a long way off and what looked like several cars. Unsure what was happening ahead, I gently shook Danny.

"Everything okay?" He yawned, waking up.

"There are people on the road ahead, what should I do?"

Danny sat up and assessed the situation. "Drive slow," he told me, "and act as normally as possible."

"What is it?" I asked alarmed.

"It's another road block."

"Maybe you should drive," I gripped the steering wheel to keep my hands from shaking.

He shook his head, "It's too late for that, if they've spotted us—and you can be sure they have— they'll want to know why we pulled over and switched places. We don't need them asking questions, better to stay as we are and act normally. Where's your passport?"

"You packed it in your bag at the falls."

Danny searched through his bag and pulled out both passports, and a small amount of cash. The closer we got to the road block the more cars we saw until eventually I was forced to wait in a line behind three others.

"Don't be nervous," Danny said. "This isn't going to be like the last time. This is only a routine check, I go through them all the time."

When it was our turn, a government soldier stepped up to our window and asked us where we were coming from and where we were going. Danny handed him our passports, first mine and then his own which contained the folded cash from his bag. He told the soldiers that I was his cousin visiting from London and that we were returning to Port Harcourt after visiting Agbokim Falls in the Calabar region. There was just

273

enough truth—and money—in Danny's story for the soldier to believe him. He gave Danny the passports back—minus the cash—and waved us through. It wasn't until we were at least a mile away that I let out a breath I wasn't aware I was holding. I stopped obsessively checking the rearview mirror and finally allowed myself to relax again.

"Never travel in this country without a bit of cash," Danny stated.

"Isn't it dangerous to bribe the soldiers?"

"This coming from the girl who offered money to the Captain to save my brother," he laughed. "Yes it's dangerous to bribe the soldiers, they can arrest you for it, but it's even more dangerous to offer them nothing. It's all about negotiating when it comes to the soldiers, and all of them want something different." He added, "Let's switch, you've been driving all day, you need a break."

I pulled the truck over on the edge of the road and slid into the passenger seat while Danny got out and walked around to the driver's side. Sleepiness settled in all at once and I leaned my head against the back of the seat.

Seconds before sleep claimed me, I heard Danny say, "Aren't you going to thank me for the driving lesson?' My eyes were closed but I could hear the humor in his voice.

"In your dreams," I mumbled.

It was the smell of smoke that woke me. I sat up and looked out the windows, searching for the source. "Where are we?" I asked.

"We're close, a few more minutes." Danny's brow was creased with worry.

The sun was setting on our right, streaking the sky with shades of orange and pink. We crept along the road approaching the village, the smoke growing thicker and burning the back of my throat. There was no question the smoke was coming from the village.

"Maybe they lit a bonfire," I said trying to reassure us both, but we knew better. Something was terribly wrong.

"Too much smoke," was all Danny managed to say.

The village came into our view and confirmed our worst fears. Several of the huts were on fire, others were only smoldering remains. Everywhere the villagers were running to the flames with buckets of water, but it was too late to put out the bonfires that were their homes. My heart sank into the pit of my stomach and panic settled in. Was anyone hurt? Were Naomi and Jim okay? Dozens of questions bounced around inside my head filling me with fear and dread.

The last few seconds it took to close the distance between us and the village felt like an eternity. As soon as Danny stopped the truck we jumped out and ran to the people nearest us. We wasted no time in joining the groups filling up the water buckets. Instead of using the pump, which would have taken too long, people—mostly the women—were filling the buckets in the river and passing them down a line to the men who then dumped the water on the fires. Our priority was to put out the fires before they could spread to the few remaining huts. In my mind I was counting of all the people I recognized. Zack was running back and forth to retrieve the empty buckets and bring them down to the river for the women to fill. Many of the other children were doing the same and, to my relief, I didn't notice any of the children I knew missing. Danny's mother, Tess, was standing next to me in the line and her husband was close by. I couldn't see Naomi, but Jim was running the heavy buckets of water straight to the huts and dumping them over the flames. It was too chaotic to check every face, but it seemed, other than the burning homes, the villagers were unscathed.

The sun had long set before the last of the fires died down. By then everyone was exhausted, soaking wet, and blackened from the ashes and smoke. Many collapsed where they were standing and gave in to their weariness and tears. Children clung to their mothers and men tried to comfort their families. I stayed near Zack and Tess until Jim and Danny found us.

Jim rushed to me and wrapped me into a tight hug, "We've been so worried about you! My mother will be so relieved to see you're safe!"

"Where is she?" I asked.

Jim's face fell, "Natalie was injured. My mother took her back to our home to care for her." Natalie, was Danny's closest friend in the village other than Jim, and as it turned out she was the only one injured in the attack.

"What happened here?" Danny asked.

"The soldiers came and set fire to the huts."

"And Natalie?"

"She was shot."

★◆★

The huts closest to the river and the furthest away from the village center—including Naomi's and Danny's huts—survived the soldier's attack. I walked beside Zack on our way to Naomi and Jim's hut. He was wearing a brave face, the same one he wore the day I met him in the marketplace, but I could tell he was terrified; whether it was the fear of what would happen to Natalie or from the shock of what he experienced, I wasn't sure. I took his hand in mine, squeezing it, and he tried to smile back. Danny and Jim walked briskly ahead of us arriving at the hut first. Zack and I followed them inside to find Natalie lying on the ground, Naomi

279

bent over her with a first aid kit, and its supplies sprawled across the floor.

"Zack, go and see how your mom is doing," I told him. The boy had seen enough already for one day and from the smell of blood that hung in the air, he didn't need to see more. He did as I said without argument and once he was gone I asked, "What can I do, Naomi?"

I moved closer for a better view and felt my stomach turn. Natalie had been shot in the lower part of her right arm, between her hand and elbow. Bone fragments jutted out at every angle and the only things still holding the arm together were a few ligaments and bits of bone. Bile rose in my throat, but I stifled it. No longer was I the girl who threw up in the Borikiri meat market, it was time for me to find my own brave face, and wear it.

Naomi motioned for us to follow her outside the hut, "The arm has to come off."

"Danny and I brought the truck back, should we drive her to the hospital in Port Harcourt?" I asked.

Naomi shook her head, "She'll never make it, she's lost too much blood, and it will become infected if we don't do something soon. The arm has to come off and it has to be now."

"What do you need?" Danny asked.

"A machete, a fire, fresh water, and an empty bucket."

"Anything else?"

"I'll need someone with a strong stomach and hands."

"I'll stay with you," I volunteered.

"Are you sure, child? This will not be a pretty thing to see," she told me.

I nodded, "I can do it."

"I'll stay too," Danny said.

Jim built up the fire and retrieved one of the many abandoned buckets lying on the ground

281

throughout the village. He left and returned with everything his mother asked for. Naomi boiled the water and used it to wash the machete, then she held the blade over the flames until it glowed orange from the heat. She nodded to Danny and me and all three of us went back inside the hut.

"What are you going to do?" Natalie asked hysterically. Horror flashed across her face when she realized the answer to her own question. "No!" She yelled. "No, please don't! Please, NO!"

"If I don't do this, you *will* die," Naomi told her.

Too weak to fight back Natalie wailed with agony.

"Hold her down," Naomi instructed Danny. He knelt next to Natalie's head and pressed his weight down onto her shoulders, pinning her in place. Naomi placed the empty bucket next to Natalie's mangled arm. To me she said, "I need you to tie this above her elbow as tightly as you can." She gave me a thick strip of cloth and I used it to make a tourniquet around Natalie's arm. "Now both of you hold onto her."

Naomi raised the machete high and brought it crashing down onto Natalie's arm in the place above the injury. My face was splashed with Natalie's blood and it took every bit of control I possessed to keep me from running out of that hut. I closed my eyes and took deep breaths, but I could still feel the movements of the machete sawing back and forth across the remaining bits of bone and flesh.

Natalie was screaming and trying to thrash, but Danny and I held her down. Danny whispered encouragements to her. "We're almost done," he said soothingly. "It's going to be okay, I promise."

I'm not sure how long it took Naomi to finish removing the arm, but all four of us were desperately needing it to be over. Naomi pressed bandages against the leftover stump and gave me a new set of directions, "Take that bucket outside and dump it on the fire.

Clean the machete and heat it up the same way I did before."

We switched places so Naomi could keep pressure on the arm. I carried the bucket to the fire without looking at its contents. I dumped the leftovers of Natalie's arm onto the hottest part of the fire and ignored the smell as I watched them burn. There was another fresh bucket of water, courtesy of Jim, and I used it to clean the blade and my hands. The water I left behind had changed to red with blood, and Jim took it away to be emptied. Danny's family, Natalie's mother, and several other villagers were sitting around the fire, but none of them would look at me. I waited for the blade to glow orange again and then I brought it back to Naomi.

She removed the bandages she was pressing against the wound and I returned to my place beside her. "Deep breaths girl," she told Natalie, though I found myself following the same advice. Naomi pressed the hot blade against the ruptured skin, melting the

284

flesh around the bone, closing the wound, and stopping the blood. The pain was too much and, mercifully, Natalie passed out. With the wound cauterized there was nothing left to do but bandage it and clean up. Danny took the machete outside and left us to finish caring for the unconscious Natalie.

"You can go now," Naomi told me. "You did good, girl. I'm proud of you." She brushed a piece of hair out of my face and added, "I'm glad you are safe and back home. Go on now, I will stay with Natalie tonight. Tell the others she has a better chance of surviving now."

I delivered Naomi's message to those gathered outside. Natalie's mother left the fire to be with her daughter and some of the villagers left to return to their families. Others stayed where they were with no place else to go. Danny was standing at the edge of the river bank alone, looking up at the stars.

"I wasn't here," he whispered.

"This isn't your fault," I said.

"I wasn't here! I could have..."

"Could have what? You think you could have stopped this? Natalie lost her arm, but her life was spared. Everyone is alive, that's all that matters."

"Maybe if I had been here instead of playing around at the waterfalls she wouldn't have lost her arm."

His comment stung. Angry and hurt I replied, "Maybe. Or maybe things would have been worse. Maybe Natalie would have been killed along with you and who knows how many others. You can play the 'maybe' game all you want, but it changes nothing. Most of the village has burned, your people, our people, have lost everything. In the morning we need to start rebuilding our homes, so you're going to have to try to snap out of it!"

I was so angry I didn't wait for a reply. I stormed off! Drained of all my energy, I collapsed in a place near the fire. A minute later I felt Zack snuggle up next to me and I wrapped my arms around him until the sun peeked above the horizon.

Chapter 13

The small fire burned out by early morning. Zack was still curled up next to me; I moved gently away so as not to wake him. I peered inside the hut, checking on Natalie who was sleeping soundly with her mother beside her and Naomi keeping watch over the both of them. When I left the hut, Naomi followed me outside.

"Will she live?" I asked.

"She has survived the injury and the night. As long as we keep the wound clean and there is no infection, she will live."

"What do we do now?"

"Now, we must wake the others."

The villagers, with the exception of Natalie and her mother, gathered around the water pump. To rebuild the homes we lost, everyone would have to take part in the process; even the smallest children could do their share. The first task was to cut down enough bamboo for at least 30 new huts. Half of the villagers followed Danny into the thickest parts of the jungle to harvest the bamboo, and the other half stayed behind with Jim to begin clearing away the remains of the old huts that were destroyed. I joined the volunteers following Danny into the jungle, with Zack right beside me, and was given my own machete for chopping down the bamboo. Zack was disappointed when no one gave him a machete, but I promised him we could take turns with mine.

The two of us found our own section of jungle, loaded with bamboo, and spent the rest of the day taking turns cutting down the tall stalks. Bamboo is very strong, I learned quickly; each swing of my blade left only a small dent and if I didn't hit the exact same spot every time it was nearly impossible to bring the giant sticks down. Between us, after several hours of practice, Zack and I were able to cut down almost enough bamboo for one small hut. We were brought water by some of the women who stayed behind in the village including Naomi whom, I expected, only wished to check on me. Danny took his break with us and when he saw our bamboo pile he couldn't hide the surprise from his face. My right hand blistered from swinging the machete and Naomi wrapped a clean piece of cloth around it to keep it from getting any worse.

Danny drove the truck as far into the jungle as he could and I helped some of the others load the bamboo we cut into the back. I found I could carry two or three of the bamboo shafts at a time and Zack managed one. We carried all of the bamboo we cut ourselves, then all of us walked back to the village behind the truck. There wasn't enough bamboo to rebuild all of the huts yet the truck was completely full; the rest would be cut down later when more was needed. This would prevent useless waste of jungle resources. The group that had remained behind clearing debris were nearly finished by the time we returned, so the next morning we were ready to start building the frames for the new huts.

The bamboo was used to frame the shape of the hut. Bamboo shafts were placed 8 to 10 inches apart all along the outer perimeter of the rounded hut. Each shaft was buried a foot deep into the ground and a V-shaped notch was carved into the top to later support the roof. The villagers again divided into different groups: some were cutting the notches into the bamboo, some were digging the 12 inch-deep holes outlining the base of the new huts, and others were already starting to build the frames of the first huts.

After the bamboo shafts were placed into the foot-deep holes, the holes were then refilled with dirt to hold them steady. Rocks were also positioned around the bamboo for extra support and stacked along the bottom edge of the frame to make the hut stronger. The rocks were recycled from the remains of the old huts, the only part the fires hadn't consumed. The vertical bamboo shafts, together with the rocks, formed the border of the hut. To build the walls the next shafts of bamboo we weaved horizontally around the vertical ones. It was difficult work forcing the bamboo to bend the way we wanted it to. I held the end of one piece of bamboo, keeping it steady, as Danny bent it around the frame; first around what would be the inner wall, and then around the outer edge, in a thatch work pattern that continued to alternate from the inner wall to the outer. The pattern looked like a grid all the way around the hut, starting from the bottom edge working its way to the top and stopping a few inches below the V notch. It was no mystery why, after a couple of days of hard work, we ran out of bamboo.

It was Danny who asked me and Zack to follow him back into the jungle. "We're out of bamboo," he told us, "and we could really use your help getting more. The two of you did a great job last time."

Zack was overjoyed to be a part of the chosen few asked to gather more bamboo. So the two of us, Danny, and some others rode in the back of the truck into the jungle. There were at least 10 men from the village with us, who spread out among the trees. Zack and I, much like the first time, picked our own little section of jungle and got to work chopping the bamboo down. I used the machete, doing the brunt of the work, while Zack carried what I cut down over to the truck. We had a great system going and in only a couple of hours we almost cleared our whole section.

As the hottest part of the day rolled in I grew tired and began to make mistakes. During one of Zack's trips to the truck I stumbled over a small rock and was barely able to keep myself from falling face-first onto the ground. The machete grazed the outside of my leg, slicing the skin just below my knee. The cut was bleeding badly and I had nothing to use to stop it. By the time Zack came running back for more bamboo, I was sitting on the ground with my dirty hand covering the cut.

"What happened?!" Zack exclaimed kneeling down next to me.

"I had a small accident with the machete, but I'm okay. It's only a small cut."

"Wait here, I'll go get Danny."

"No!" I grabbed his arm to stop him from leaving. "I'm fine really. We don't need to tell anyone."

"But..."

"No one else needs to know," I said firmly.

"What should I do?" He asked.

"I need to stop the bleeding, do you have your bandana with you?" He nodded and pulled the red bandana he always carried out from his pocket. "If I tie it around my leg I think I'll be okay."

I used the bandana to clean the blood from my leg and my hand, then pressed it hard against the wound. The cut wasn't very deep and only hurt a little bit. I wrapped the bandana around my leg and tied it tight. The bleeding stopped within a couple of minutes and Zack helped me to my feet.

"You need to go get it cleaned," Zack told me.

"I will later. It can wait a couple more hours." I added, "Why don't you take the machete for a while, I could use a break."

Delighted, the boy took the machete from me and picked up where I left off. I watched him work and then together we carried our bamboo pile over to the truck. Danny was standing there with a fresh bucket of water for us to drink. He gave it to his brother first and I continued to load the bamboo into the back of the truck on my own. Danny brought the water over to me and ordered me to drink. I tilted the bucket over my mouth and let the cool water run down my throat.

I tried to give the bucket back to Danny but he shook his head. "Drink more. Your face is bright red and you look exhausted, you need to keep hydrated."

I did as instructed, embarrassed by his description of my appearance. I couldn't and didn't want to imagine what I must have looked like. I was a mess; there was dirt caked beneath my finger nails, my hair was tied back with several rebellious strays falling into my face, and apparently my face was bright red from the heat. Not to mention the cut I was hiding on the side of my leg, which was beginning to throb painfully.

Danny spoke to me as I drank from the bucket, "I've been wanting to apologize to you for what I said when we got back. I was angry for not being here and after what we had to do for Natalie..." he paused. "I'm sorry. I'm glad we went to the falls and I'm glad that you were with me when we got here. You were really great you know, with the Natalie thing, and you've been a lot of help with the building. You were right telling me to snap out of it and focus on helping our families. I guess what I'm trying to say is...I mean what I really mean is..." he stopped struggling with the words.

"I believe the words you're looking for are, 'thank you,'" I said.

"I guess you're right," Danny laughed. "Thank you, Mari."

"You're welcome," I gave the bucket back to him and turned to walk away. The pain in my leg was increasing and as I stepped forward I stumbled a little.

Danny caught me by the arm with an angry look on his face.

"What's wrong with your leg?" He asked roughly.

"It's nothing, I bumped it with the machete. It's only a scratch."

"Let me see it."

"Really it's fine, nothing to worry about."

Ignoring me, Danny ripped the bandana from my leg and gasped, "That is *not* a scratch, Mari! What is wrong with you? How many times do you have to be told how dangerous an injury like this can be? Why didn't you tell me?"

"It's not a big deal, it's only a small cut. I planned to take care of it as soon as we were done."

Danny walked away from me shaking his head in frustration, "Get in the truck."

"Danny its fine..."

"Get into the truck," he said more forcefully, then added, "you too Zack."

Danny drove us back to the village and straight over to Naomi. The men who had stayed in the village unloaded the bamboo from the truck and stacked it next to the huts while Naomi went to find the first aid kit she kept in her home. Danny made me sit down on the ground and sent Zack for water. On our short drive to the village Danny yelled at Zack for not telling anyone about my leg. He said the boy knew better than that and should have been ashamed of himself for helping keep my secret. I tried to stand up for Zack and tell Danny it wasn't his fault, but Danny refused to hear anything I said.

When Zack gave Danny the water, he poured it over my leg washing the dirt and grime away. I winced when he poured the water into the cut and Danny shook his head at me again. Naomi returned with the first aid kit and took over.

"Don't you dare let either of them out of your sight," Danny told Naomi before leaving us again. "Neither of them are to leave this village again today."

I felt like a child being put in a time-out, which left me feeling small and embarrassed. The cut stung as Naomi cleaned and bandaged it. She too, lectured Zack and me about our foolishness in keeping secrets, taking Danny's side against us.

"I'm sorry," I told her. "Don't blame Zack, it was my fault, I begged him not to say anything."

"I do not understand you, girl," Naomi chided me. "You should know better by now."

"I know, I just didn't want to be a nuisance. I'm trying really hard to be helpful, I'm tired of feeling so useless."

Naomi sighed and shook her head, "You are not useless, girl. You made a mistake, now learn from it."

"What am I supposed to do now? Danny has banned me from helping, but I don't want to sit around watching while the others are all working."

Naomi packed up the first aid kit and said, "Danny cannot stop you from helping with the work if that is what you really want to do."

"It is," I told her. "But what can I do?"

"Come," she helped me to my feet, "and I will show you."

I followed her, with Zack trailing behind me, to a group of older women too frail to over exert themselves in the heat, who were sitting in a circle with palm leaves scattered all around them. When the women saw us approaching they widened their circle to fit the three of us, and we were each given our own palm leaf. All of the palm leaves were split in half down the middle and separated into two different piles—one for the right-side, and one for the left. Naomi laid her leaf flat on the ground in front of her and motioned for Zack and me to watch. She counted over to the fifth leaflet—the long strands that hung from the spine—and then weaved it backwards, over and under the first four leaflets she had skipped. Then she took the seventh leaflet and weaved it backwards. She continued all the way across, continuing the pattern. When she finished the first row of weaving she stopped and pointed at the palm leaf on my lap.

"Now you try," she said.

The thatch-work pattern was simple and once I got the hang of it I was able to move swiftly as though I'd been doing it for years. The other women gossiped while they did their work, talking about people and places I'd never heard of, and I found their voices soothing while my hands busily weaved the leaflets over and under, over and under. There was an easy rhythm to the work. I finished my first palm leaf and saw a few of the others nod in approval. Naomi showed me how to weave the ends of the leaflets back through the pattern so my work would not unravel, and then I was handed a brand new leaf.

"How did you finish yours?" Zack asked sitting beside me. I hadn't noticed him working on his own leaf and was surprised to find how much better his came out than mine.

"Good job, child," Naomi told him.

I put my new leaf down and showed him how Naomi taught me to finish off the pattern and he quickly finished his first leaf too. He put down his work and left to get water for our little group so we could stay hydrated as the sun beat down on us. Our pile of finished palm leaves grew as we worked, until we had enough for nearly two hut roofs.

Natalie, who had kept her distance from everyone since her injury, approached our small circle and was happily invited to join. Zack gave her his spot next to me and moved to the other side of Naomi. Natalie sat down, but said nothing when one of the women gave her a palm leaf. She stared at it on the ground in front of her for a long time before reaching for the first of the leaflets. She tried to weave it through the others but struggled because she was unable to hold the leaf steady. The leaf kept moving, and her hand was working against what little weaving she managed to complete come undone. Each time one of the leaves came loose Natalie grew more and more frustrated.

I wanted to help her but was afraid she wouldn't let me. Instead I asked her the dumbest question I could've possibly asked: "How are you, Natalie?"

The girl stopped her attempt at weaving and glared at me. "How do you think I am?"

"Is there anything I can do to help?"

"Don't you think you've done enough already?' She snapped. I realized she was probably thinking back to the moment when I held her down while Naomi hacked away what was left of her arm.

"I'm sorry," I replied and lowered my head down over my work. Out of the corner of my eye I saw Naomi giving Natalie her evil eye.

After a few seconds Natalie said, "I'm sorry, Mari, it's not your fault I'm angry. Thank you for offering to help me, but I need to try to do this on my own."

Natalie and I did not know each other very well, but in that moment I understood her. The two of us were a lot alike, both stubborn in our own ways. She took a breath then tried her weaving again with the same result. She tried a few more times and at last gave up throwing her leaf down in the middle of the circle.

"I can't do this!" She yelled, covering her face with her hand to hide her tears.

"Yes you can," I picked up her leaf and returned it to the ground in front of her.

"You don't understand. I have to re-learn how to do everything. I can't do it!"

I squatted down in front of her while the others watched, and forced her hand away from her face, "Yes you can," I told her firmly.

"How?"

I stood up and walked away from the group. I could feel their eyes watching curiously as I left them and could hear that Natalie had stopped crying. I quickly searched the village with a plan forming. I found what I was looking for near one of the new huts and returned to the weaving group armed with two medium-sized rocks. The women, Natalie included, eyed me strangely as I placed one of the rocks on top of the hard stem of the palm leaf. I used the second rock on the opposite end to hold down the leaflets so that they would stay straight like the strings on a loom.

Natalie caught on to the idea and her eyes lit up with hope. She pulled one of the leaflets loose and weaved it over and under the next several. The method wasn't perfect, but the rocks held the palm leaf steady enough that weaving became possible. Naomi looked on proudly as Natalie finished weaving an entire row, and the others clapped their hands excitedly.

"You can," I told Natalie, "because I'm going to help you."

<u>Chapter 14</u>

It was an all-out war. I hid behind one of the huts, knowing it was only a matter of time before they caught me. I carefully peered around the corner then dashed quickly over to the cover of the next hut. I stopped to catch my breath, *I don't think anyone saw me,* I thought. I needed to keep moving, that was the most important thing. No one could catch me if I kept moving. I took a deep breath and ran, but I made a crucial mistake: I forgot to check if the path between the huts was clear. I ran straight into the hands of my enemy.

I threw my hands up in surrender and began to back away, "I swear I didn't mean to."

"Oh really?"

"Don't do it!" I begged. "Don't you dare…" My words were too late. The fresh ball of mud had already left Danny's hand and was soaring towards my face. I tried to duck, but the mud still found me.

Work on the new huts was almost complete with only one last ingredient needed: mud. The villagers used their hands and rudimentary tools to dig a large hole, which became the mixing bowl for the final part of our building project. Water was poured into the hole along with dried grass—the exact recipe being 1 part dried grass to every 2 parts mud. That's when the fun started. We used our feet and hands to mix the dirt, water, and grass together, creating the thick mud needed to form the walls around the bamboo frames we had already built.

I grabbed a bucket and filled it with the mud mixture, following everyone over to the new huts. The mud was taken in handfuls and thrown from a short distance, against the bottom of the frame where the wall would be the thickest. People worked on both the insides and the outsides at the same time, working their way from the bottom, up, flinging the mud against the rocks and the bamboo shafts. It was another hot day, and I could feel my face flush with color, but the work was so much fun I hardly noticed.

The mud war was my fault. I had a very large handful of mud that I threw at the hut we were working on, but my aim was way off. My mud ball hit Danny square on the side of his face. Thinking that I had done it on purpose—and subconsciously I probably did— Danny retaliated with his own handful of mud which missed me and hit Zack. Zack didn't miss when he threw his own mud ball, hitting Danny right in the middle of his chest. The three of us stood there eyeing each other, then Zack and I bolted. Danny chased after us and the mud war began. Soon everyone had chosen a side and mud was flying from all directions.

Zack and I were separated. I was on my own and running desperately low on mud. It was my journey back to the mud pit that resulted in Danny finding me. His mud-missile hit me in the back of the head as I tried to run away. I was aiming for the mud pit as I ran but my leg was sore and Danny was too fast for me, overtaking me a few feet away from my goal. He grabbed my arm and stopped. We stood facing one another and I wasn't sure what to do. There was still a little bit of mud in the bottom of my bucket, so I lifted it up and dumped it onto his head.

Danny didn't react for a few seconds, letting the mud ooze down his head, but then he rushed me, picking me up in a fireman's hold over his shoulder, while I kicked and yelled at him to put me down. He carried me over to the hole and threw me down into the fresh gooey mud. I landed on my back, making a sucking noise as I started to sink. Danny stood above me grinning, proud of himself and thinking he had won. He turned his back to me and I reached up and grabbed his foot, pulling him into the pit beside me. I sat up and looked at him lying there in the mud and started to laugh. Once I started laughing I couldn't stop.

"What're you laughing at?" Danny asked sitting up. The mud fell off him in lumps making me laugh even harder. Danny laughed too. "So you think this is funny, huh?" He threw more mud at me and the next thing I knew we were rolling around in the mud laughing and squealing like a couple of little kids.

Exhausted, we pulled ourselves out of the pit and lay on our backs on the ground. I stared up at the sky, at the few small clouds rolling in from the distance, and felt Danny lace his fingers through mine. I closed my eyes, completely content, and drifted off into a nap, the sun baking the mud onto my skin.

A small raindrop landed on my face, waking me. I arrived in Nigeria during the dry season and had not yet seen a single drop of rain. Danny stood and pulled me up with him, keeping my hand in his. Without warning, that one small raindrop turned into a torrential downpour and the people opened their arms wide, welcoming the new rainy season. My natural reaction to so much rain was to run for cover, but I looked at the people around me and instead of seeking shelter, they were using the fresh water to wash themselves clean of the mud caked onto their bodies. The mud war was forgotten as buckets caught the rain and were dumped over people's heads. Danny poured a bucket of water over my head and I scrubbed the dirt out of my hair. I cleaned my clothes as best I could, but I knew they would forever remain stained from the mud.

A sudden wave of nausea came over me as I showered in the rain. My leg was throbbing, the bandage red and soggy. The cut had been bothering me for a couple of days, though I did my best keeping it hidden. I swallowed back the nausea and tried to shake myself out of it. Danny was pouring another bucket of water over Zack's head and I smiled when he looked at me.

"How's that feel?" Danny asked about the shower.

"Amazing," I replied. "I didn't think I would ever feel this clean again."

"Don't worry, you'll be dirty again in no time," Danny grinned.

"How long will the rain last?"

"A few months. There will be a couple of hours of dry every day, but for the most part it will stay like this."

"It rained all the time back in London, but nothing like this. It was usually grey and dreary. Sometimes it would rain hard, but it wouldn't last long."

I thought back to my home in London. I would spend the worst rainy days in the house, curled up in my mother's sitting room with a good book and a hot chocolate, which Joseph always made for me. Ruth would tidy the house and Craig would study in his room. Sometimes the four of us would start a fire in the large fireplace downstairs and play cards until the late hours of the night. Other times we would have movie marathons, watching all of our favorites together. In my mind I drifted back there and could see Joseph's smiling face and Craig cheating at cards while Ruth scolded him. A small part of me was missing home.

"Are you alright?" Danny asked me. He woke me from my day dream, a look of concern on his face.

"I feel a little tired," I told him. He touched my forehead with the back of his hand.

"You're burning up! Come on, let's get you out of this rain."

Danny helped me back to Naomi's hut and sat me down on my straw bed. "Where are your dry clothes?" I pointed to my back pack lying on the ground and he brought it over to me. He took out a new set of clothes, "Put these on."

"I'm not going to change in front of you!"

"Relax, I'm going outside, just call me when you're done."

He left and I peeled off my wet clothes. I slipped into my dry shorts and was barely able to pull my shirt over my head. Standing up to put on the clothes wore me out, all my strength was leaving me. In a weak voice I called out Danny's name, hoping he could hear me over the heavy rain. I felt as if I was going to fall, and then I felt Danny's hands catching me. He gently lowered me down onto the straw mattress again so that I was leaning with my back against the mud wall. He noticed the dirty bandages around my leg and furrowed his brow.

"We need to change these bandages," he said.

No, I thought, but I was too weak to say no. I felt him pulling at the bandages and leaned my head against the wall, closing my eyes. When the last of the bandages fell away I heard Danny's sharp intake of breath.

"Oh no," he said. He repeated it over and over, "No, no, no, no, no."

I didn't need to open my eyes; I knew what it looked like. The cut on my leg was swollen, bright red, and oozing yellowish pus. I could smell the stench of it beginning to fill the hut. Red lines were inching their way up my leg.

I could hear their voices, though the world around me turned dark.

"It's too late, the infection is in her bloodstream," said Naomi's voice

Something cool was placed on my burning forehead, "She's on fire." Natalie's voice came from beside me.

"Her pulse is racing," I felt Tess gripping my wrist tightly.

"What do we do?" Danny asked.

"She needs antibiotics, they're the only thing that can save her now," Tess answered. "We should take her to the hospital."

"Port Harcourt is too far, and there's the risk that they'll turn her away," Naomi said.

"It's our only option," Tess argued.

"What about the rebel camp?" Natalie asked.

"Too dangerous," Naomi replied.

"No. Natalie is right. The rebels have medicines and they're closer than Port Harcourt," Danny said.

"What makes you think they'll give you what you need?" Naomi asked.

"Because George will never let Lila's daughter die." There was a pause, then Danny added, "If I'm going to do this, it has to be *now*. Every second we waste there's a greater chance Mari won't make it."

"Go then," Naomi told him. "Be as quick as you can."

The air around me stirred and Danny's voice was in my ear, "Mari, I need you to fight. Fight as hard as you can, I'll be back soon." His lips brushed the side of my cheek. To Natalie he said, "Try to keep her temperature down, it might slow the infection."

"I will do my best for her," she replied. "Hurry back."

I was in my mother's sitting room. She was curled up in her chair by the window, her favorite book open on her lap. She looked up at me as I moved closer, her smile turned into a frown.

"Mother?"

"Mari. What are you doing here?" She rose from the chair and wrapped me in her arms. "You shouldn't be here, my love."

"How did I get here? Am I dreaming?"

She brushed a strand of hair away from my face, "Yes love, you're dreaming. You're sick, Mari, you have a fever."

I remembered nothing of being sick, "Mother, I'm in Nigeria. I found Naomi and her son. I've met Ken Saro-Wiwa and Soboma George. I'm living in your village!"

"I know my love. I'm so proud of you."

"I know the truth. You went to London to stop Father from destroying the Ogoni lands. You only married him so you could spy on him."

"No Mari that was not the only reason. I loved him and I believed that once he realized what he was doing he would stop. I thought he was capable of change, but I was wrong."

"You were going to leave him, weren't you? You were taking me and Craig and you were going back to your home."

"Yes, I was."

"What happened? Why didn't we leave? How did you get so sick?" I was upset, almost yelling at her; at last the pieces of her past were falling into place.

"Mari, calm down!" She shook me. My skin felt like it was on fire. "Listen to me, we don't have much time. If you don't wake up soon, you won't wake up at all."

"You were never sick were you?"

"You have to go back Mari. You have to finish what I started. Stop your Father. You and Craig are the only ones who can do it."

"Did Father poison you?"

"You need to wake up, Mari!"

"Did he kill you?!"

"Wake up Mari!"

My mother's face faded and blurred, "Mother tell me! Did he kill you?!"

"Wake up Mari!" The voice no longer belonged to my mother. "Please wake up, Mari. Please!" Danny begged.

The world around me shifted. I was in Naomi's hut, lying on my bed, my skin hot but no longer burning.

I blinked my eyes open, my vision a bit blurry. I tried again. Danny was sitting on the ground next to me, squeezing my wrist in his hand. Zack was watching from the doorway.

I was so horribly thirsty. My throat was so dry that when I tried to speak it came out as a noiseless moan.

"Mari?"

I closed my eyes again, wanting to drift off into my dream world so I could see my mother's face one more time.

"Come on Mari, open your eyes," Danny was shaking me. "It's time to wake up."

"Danny?" I cracked my eyes open.

"I'm right here, Mari. Zack, go get Naomi, tell her Mari's waking up."

A Rebel Star

My throat was unbearably dry, "Water!" I croaked.

"And bring us some water!" Danny called after Zack.

I tried to lift myself so I could sit up, but I was too weak.

"Easy now," Danny said supporting my shoulders. He helped me sit up and lean against the hut. "Are you alright like this?"

I nodded. Before I could ask how long I'd been unconscious, Zack came barging in carrying a full bucket of water with Naomi trailing behind him. Danny held the bucked, lifting it so I could drink. The water soothed my painful throat and cracked lips. Danny put the bucket aside and left me and Naomi alone.

"What happened?" I asked.

"The infection in your leg spread into your bloodstream. It's very common and is the reason you

324

have to keep all your wounds clean. Maybe now you'll understand," Naomi snapped at me.

"I'm sorry." My mind floated back to my dream. My mother told me I was sick, that if I didn't wake up I might not at all. Was I really that close to dying? I know it was only a dream but it was so real. I could feel my mother's arms as she embraced me. It was my dream that helped me put together the remaining parts of Mother's story, my subconscious mind drawing conclusions to facts I hadn't realized I already knew. All of it was summed up in one important, inarguable truth: My father murdered my mother.

Naomi sighed and sat down next to me, "You scared me girl, don't you ever do that to me again. I thought we lost you. If it wasn't for Danny we would have. That boy drove faster than I ever thought that truck could go, bartered with the rebels for antibiotics, and hasn't left your side since he got back. He saved your life, Mari."

I let Naomi's words sink in without reply. Did Danny really care about me that much? There were times when he irritated me so badly that I couldn't stand looking at him, but there were so many more times—I was beginning to notice—that I was excited by the thought of seeing him and spending time with him. Danny was nothing like the guys I dated in London, guys like Brian, who cared more about themselves than the people they supposedly loved. Danny was not only capable of taking care of himself, but also his family. He helped feed the village and flirted with danger as he offered aid to the rebels. He saved my life from soldiers, kept me alive in the jungle and the rebel camp, only to turn around and save me again! All along I thought he was only tolerating me for the sake of Naomi and Jim and his brother; it never once crossed my mind that maybe he cared for me, myself. Or maybe it was me who cared for him.

"Can you help me up?" I asked Naomi.

"You should rest," she replied.

"I've been resting for days, I need to stand up."

Naomi pulled me up to my feet and steadied me as a wave of dizziness hit me. "You're not strong enough yet."

"I only need a few minutes, then I'll come right back and sleep as long as you want me to, I promise."

It was dusk, the sun setting behind clouds of orange and pink. Jim was sitting by the fire with Zack, working on his fishing nets.

"It is good to see you standing, Mari," Jim smiled. I put a hand on his shoulder and squeezed. I ruffled Zack's hair with my other hand and kissed the top of his blonde head.

"Where's Danny?" I asked.

Jim pointed, "He's down by the river."

I could see Danny's silhouette in the dim light. My limbs were stiff, my leg still sore, so I moved slowly, limping towards the river bank. I reached out and gently touched his arm to let him know I was there, and partly to help me keep my balance.

"Mari, what are you doing up? You should be resting," his face was twisted with worry.

"It's alright, Naomi gave me permission as long as I'm back in the hut in a few minutes."

The lines on his face softened, "I'm glad you're okay. You scared everyone. You scared *me*."

"You saved my life...again."

"Yeah well, let's make that the last time I need to. No more accidents Mari, you have to be more careful. You can't just keep..."

He never finished his sentence. I stopped his mouth with mine, his gorgeous green eyes filled with concern too much of a temptation for me to resist. When I at last pulled away from him, after an abrupt "Gross!" coming from Zack, Danny was smiling.

"You know," he said, "I would have settled for a simple, 'thank you.'"

Then he kissed me again.

Chapter 15

I regained most of my strength in about a week, spending only a few short hours outside the hut every day. Zack never left my side for a second, he even slept on the ground next to me each night as if he was afraid I would become sick again. Danny checked on me regularly in the mornings and then again in the late afternoons. When I asked him where he went everyday he told me that he used the leftover money from the rebels to buy food and supplies for the other Ogoni villages.

"Maybe one day I'll take you with me," he offered.

"I'd really like that," I told him.

Natalie and her mother, and Danny's parents, Tess and Barry, were also constant visitors, along with some of the older women from our weaving group. Tess hugged me, squeezing me tight, and Natalie told me how glad she was that I survived. Barry pat me on the back and congratulated me on surviving what he called my first illness.

"*First* illness?" I found his comment disturbing.

He laughed, a sound that came from deep within his belly, "I'm surprised you haven't gotten sick sooner! Your body isn't used to this kind of environment, I'm sure this won't be the last infection or disease you catch. All the same you gave us quite a scare young lady. I think I speak for everyone when I say we are relieved to see you back on your feet."

"I have your son to thank for that," I replied.

"He's a good boy, our Danny. I think he's quite taken with you," Barry winked. I smiled to myself and tried to hide the blush that was creeping up my cheeks.

Nighttime was my favorite part of the day as everyone came over to eat around our fire. We ate and we laughed, and although Craig, Ruth, and Joseph were missing from my life, I knew I had found my family. My home.

"I'm going into Port Harcourt, but I shouldn't be long," Danny told me one morning. He kissed me and said he would come see me as soon as he got back. Zack, finally deciding I was well enough to leave on my own, went into the city with his brother.

I was in for another one of my days wandering around the hut with nothing to do—work on the huts was finally finished, and Naomi still wouldn't let me help her with her daily work even though I was better. Jim was sitting on the end of his boat on the river bank, prepping his nets for another day of fishing.

He smiled as I approached him, "Are you going out on the water today?"

Jim nodded, "I probably won't catch anything, but I must try."

"Could I come with you? I haven't been out on the river yet."

"Sure, grab the other end of this net and hop into the boat."

I climbed into the front of the old, small boat and Jim pushed it into the water, jumping into the back at the last second. The motor started with a loud cough, then pushed us forward down the river. A warm breeze blew off the water, pushing the hair back from my face.

"So where do you usually go to fish?" I asked above the engine noise. "Do you have a special spot?"

"I try to go where there is less oil in the water."

"How can you tell?" I was looking at the water surface closest to the boat.

Jim pointed towards the river banks and told me to look closely. All along the edge of the river bank there were rainbows of color glowing in the water, and underneath the colors the water was dark and thick. I looked on both sides of the river and then again at the water around the boat; all of it looked the same. I had an urge to run my hand in the water beside me, so I dipped my fingertips in and immediately pulled them back. My fingers were black, covered in oil and sludge. Jim tossed me a rag and I wiped my fingers clean.

"This is disgusting, Jim. You can't fish here, nothing alive will be safe enough to eat."

"We have to go much farther downstream to find clear water."

I watched the black waters flow under the boat. The bodies of fish floated by us, their cloudy, dead eyes staring up at me, accusing me. *This is your fault,* they seemed to say as the oil clogged their gills. How many thousands of fish, birds, and other animals had my father murdered? How many people? Throughout my time spent in the village I saw the damage oil pollution caused. I saw the smoke and the flames from gas flaring. I saw the fields where people used to grow their food, seeping with so much oil, that the land could no longer be farmed. I saw the polluted waters before me, and Jim's net which almost always came back empty. I saw the Ogoni people, who lived there. I witnessed them overcome every challenge nature, Nigeria's corrupt government, and my father threw at them, and I knew in that moment on Jim's boat, that I more than loved them: I admired them and their struggle. My eyes brimmed with tears, a few escaping down my cheeks.

"Sometimes it's better, sometimes it's worse," Jim interrupted my thoughts. "Ah, here we go, there's a clear spot over there."

I looked ahead to the place he was pointing. There was a section of water, much lighter than the rest of the river. He stopped the boat and let it drift into the clear water.

"Would you like to cast the net?" Jim asked.

I cleaned my eyes, "How do I do it?"

"Stand up slowly."

"What if I tip the boat?"

Jim smiled, "You won't. She's sturdy this old girl. Go nice and slow and you'll be fine."

I eased myself off my seat, standing as carefully as I could. The boat rocked gently, but remained upright, "Now what?"

"Take the net," he handed me a section of netting, "and throw it as far into the clean water as you can. Try not to get too close to the river bank or the net will get tangled."

I lifted as much of the heavy net as I could and threw it out into the clear water. To my disappointment, the net did not go very far. Jim laughed and used a rope that was attached to the net to pull it back.

"Try again, you want to throw it so that the weights around the edges of the net spread out evenly in the water. The wider the net lands the more you catch."

The net was heavy with water when I tried the second time, but with Jim's instructions I was able to throw it farther. Each time I threw the net Jim would pull it back quickly with the rope. Fishing was hard work—the muscles in my arms and back were sore after only a few minutes—and offered no reward in the oil polluted Nigerian waters. I cast the net into the water more times than I could count and every time it came back empty.

"Why do you keep coming out here, Jim?" I asked frustrated. "It's pointless. There are no fish in this water."

"Because there is always hope Mari," he motioned for me to sit back down. "One day the fish will come back and until then I cannot give up. I remember fishing with my father when I was young. He would bring me with him and let me cast the net out into the water. The pollution wasn't as bad back then. Some days the nets were empty, other times the nets were so heavy with fish we could barely pull them back into the boat. We sold the fish in the villages and the market and always charged less than all the other fishers. My father was a great man."

"He sounds like it. I wish I could have met him."

"Sometimes, I am almost glad he's not here. I miss him, but I am glad he didn't live to see the polluted water and the empty nets. Fishing was his life, it would have hurt him deeply to see it this way."

"How did he die?"

"The same way most fishermen do. He dove into the water to untangle his net and never came back up. It was one of the few days I wasn't with him; he was all alone."

"I'm so sorry, Jim. He would have been proud of you."

To change the subject Jim asked if I would like to pull the net back. I gripped the rope with both hands and pulled as hard as I could. The net was heavier in the water, but because it was empty the weight was manageable for me. I nearly had all of it back in the boat when I heard a splash.

"Quick, pull the net in!" Jim exclaimed. We worked together to bring the rest of the net in, and in the very end we found five medium-sized, silver fish tangled in the net. With the skill of a fisherman, Jim quickly untangled the fish and placed them in a bucket of river water. Then he looked up at me and said:

"You see Mari, there is always hope."

"Naomi!" I shouted when Jim landed the boat on the river bank. "Come see what we've got!" I jumped out of the boat and went running to find Naomi.

"What are you yelling about, girl?" She asked emerging from the hut. "And where have you been all day?"

I was out of breath, "Jim and I caught five fish!"

To prove it, Jim put the bucket of fresh fish down in front of her. Naomi's eyes lit up and she declared, "I know what we'll be eating for dinner tonight."

I heard Jim's truck approaching from the village and my heart pounded excitedly. Danny was home. I waited impatiently for him to park the truck and climb out, then I pounced on him. I flung myself into his arms, squealing in delight.

"I've only been gone a few hours," Danny laughed. "Did you really miss me that much?"

"I have a surprise for you," I led him over to the bucket of fish.

"How did you…"

"Jim took me out on the river today and taught me how to fish."

"You did this?"

"She sure did," Jim answered, winking at me.

"That's amazing!"

Zack wrapped his arm around my waist and said, "We have a surprise for you too."

"Really? What kind of surprise?" I looked at Danny.

"Go see for yourself, it's in the back of the truck." I raced over to the truck, hearing my surprise long before I saw it. I could hardly believe my ears.

"Get me out of this thing," the voice said. "This is disgusting."

I knew that voice, and even though I hadn't heard it for months, I recognized it immediately.

"Craig?!"

"Hey sis," Craig was standing next to the truck, looking miserable and happy all at the same time. I ran to him, forgetting everyone else, and threw my arms around his neck.

"What are you doing here? How did you find me?"

"It's a long story," he laughed and hugged me back.

"I can't believe you're here! I have so much to tell you!"

"I want to hear everything, but Mari I need to talk to you."

"Come and meet everyone first, we can talk later," I took his hand the way I used to when we were young, and dragged him over to Naomi. "Craig this is Naomi, she was Mother's best friend."

Naomi studied him nearly the same way she studied me the day I arrived. She put her hands on his shoulders and held him at arm's length away from her, "You have so much of Lila in you, much more than I expected. I'm so happy to meet you at last."

"I'm glad to meet you too," Craig replied.

Having already met Danny and Zack in the Borikiri Market, I introduced him to Jim next, who happily shook his hand and welcomed him. There was something strange about the way Craig was acting; cold and businesslike, almost like our father. I could sense something was wrong, even Danny was looking at me strangely.

"Has something happened?" I asked my brother. "Are Ruth and Joseph alright?"

"They're fine, they send their love. Everyone's fine...but, I really need to talk to you." He turned to the others. "I'm really sorry, I don't mean to be rude, but I must speak with my sister privately."

No one moved from where they were standing. "Please," Craig begged them and me.

"Anything you have to say, you can say in front of them," I told him, planting my feet firmly on the ground to make my point.

"Mari, he's here."

A lump formed in the back of my throat, "What?"

"Father," Craig paused, "he's here."

"The minute I discovered you were missing, I begged Father to search for you. He refused. He's known all along where you were and was perfectly content with leaving you here. He said you had made your decision and wouldn't hear any more about it."

"Then why is here now?" I asked.

"Because of this." Craig handed me a folded piece of newspaper from his pocket. On it was an article entitled *Where's Mari?* with a small photo of me at a social event from the previous year. "At first, no one really noticed you were gone except for Brian and Kirstin, but months have gone by and people are starting to ask questions. Go ahead, read it." He pointed to the article in my hands.

Where's Mari?

By Michael P.

Do you remember the days as a child when your mother handed you a picture of a busy city street, bustling with people of all sorts and left you with the frustrating, yet exciting, task of locating that one man in the crowd wearing a red and white striped shirt and hat? Your job was to find the one among the many who stood out, yet was so carefully hidden right underneath your nose.

What was it about Wally that made us keep searching for him? While I cannot answer as to Wally's character, I found myself thrown into his world once again only this time with a new question: Where's Mari?

I've been pouring over hundreds of pictures, all from this year's finest social events, for days, but it wasn't until late last night, leaning over my office desk covered in a collage of photos that I realized there was one face missing. Marienela, preferring to be called Mari by those closest to her, is the daughter of that wealthy oil tycoon we all love to hate, yet whose money will always be welcome; but she is, by far, the most interesting young person of London's social elite. Always ready for her close up, dressed to the nines, and on the arm of the most handsome man in the room— or so I've been told by those jealous few when they attended these occasions—I have never known Mari to be missing from a single one of these events, let alone a whole season's worth. Where is she?

A Rebel Star

After hours of searching, hundreds of unanswered questions, and several refused interviews with her own father, I am now extremely concerned about the well-being of our dear Mari. What has happened to her? Has she gone on a secret vacation to get away from us all or on some trip of discovery to a faraway land? If that's the case then why does her father refuse to answer my questions about her? Or is it something much darker that has taken her, such as foul play? I dare not allow my mind to wander to the terrible possibilities of her disappearance. One thing I know for sure, Mari is not in London.

Mari, if you are out there and this article miraculously finds its way into your hands, your audience wants you to know you are missed. Send us word that you are safe, and come back to us. Until then I will continue to search for your face amongst the many in the crowd, like I did as a child with the man in the red and white stripes.

A Rebel Star

"I think the article speaks for itself," Craig said when I finished. "I doubt I have to tell you how angry it made Father."

"Angry enough to come all the way to Nigeria," I replied.

"This makes him look bad, Mari. I mean, *'foul play?'* It's practically suggesting he murdered you!"

"Who's Wally?" Naomi asked.

I nearly laughed, "You've never heard of *Where's Wally?* He's a cartoon character who's hidden in the middle of some chaotic scene and you have to try to find him. It's surprisingly difficult."

"The better question is," Danny interrupted, "who is Michael P.?"

"He's just some reporter with a soft spot for Mari," Craig replied.

"He's not just *some* reporter," I snapped. "He's a nice man who writes puff pieces for the newspaper, anything about the rich and famous."

"He's a glorified tabloid writer," Craig muttered, "Who often has to write articles of apology or retraction. He doesn't use his last name in order to keep himself anonymous, because not everyone likes what he has to say." Turning back to me, Craig said, "Anyway I'm here to deliver a message to you."

"What does Father want from me?" I asked.

"He wants you to fix this."

"And how does he propose I do that?"

"He wants you to come home and do an interview with Michael P., show your face around town, put an end to all these rumors."

"And then what?"

"Then you can go back to living your normal life at home. Don't you want that?"

I thought about it for a moment. Any other time in my life I would have desperately wanted exactly what Craig and my father were offering, but after everything I had seen and everything I had been through I knew that my old life was over. I would never be able to go back. I can't leave Craig. There's nothing left for me in London. This *is* my home now."

My brother was dumbfounded, "Mari, I don't understand. Why would you want to stay here? You can't live like this"

"I *have* been living like this."

"Mari, you have to come back with me, it's been awful since you left. Father has been worse than ever, I can't go back to him alone. Please, come home with me."

"I'm sorry Craig, I really am, but I can't. I'm staying here."

"Mari, please..."

"She's given you her answer," Danny cut him off, taking my side.

Craig slumped his shoulders and covered his face with his hands, "You don't understand. You can't stay here."

"What do you mean?" I asked taking a step towards him.

He lifted his eyes to mine and said, "You are all in danger."

Chapter 16

"What do you mean danger?" Danny narrowed his eyes at Craig and crossed his arms over his chest. "What kind of danger?"

Craig paused to gather his thoughts and I used the moment to study him. He was sweating—from stress or from the heat, or both I wasn't sure—and he looked worn out; there were dark circles under his brown eyes and his skin was a bit pale.

"A few days after the article was released," he started "Father came to me and said he found you and that you were in danger. He told me he received information from one of his sources here that the village you have been living in is going to be attacked."

"What source?" Danny raised his voice. "How could they get that information?"

Craig ignored him, "Father knew you wouldn't come back with him so he sent me to talk to you. There is a rebel uprising coming, and the Ogoni villages are going to end up right in the middle of it. If you die here after everyone has read this article, it will look very bad for Father. He is desperate to bring you back to London safely. He'll give you anything you want if you come home with us."

"A rebel attack makes no sense," Danny argued. "George's fight is with the oil company and the government, not with us. He has no need to attack the villages. And none of the other rebel groups have ever bothered us before, they have no reason to. We have nothing they could possibly want."

"My Father is lying," I told them. "He's trying to manipulate me into leaving by convincing me I'm in danger and that he's the only one who can protect me, so that I'll return to London and tell everyone that he's my savior. The press would eat it up and he would look like a hero in the papers."

"I don't think he's bluffing," Craig said. "He seemed certain that the villages are going to be attacked. He seemed..." Craig stopped.

"What?"

"Smug," Craig finished. "What if he's right, Mari? What if an attack *is* going to happen? You're gambling with your life if you stay here."

I stepped away from them, closer to the fire, so I could think. Craig's story made no sense, there were too many holes and loose ends; there was something big missing. My father would never have given Craig the full story or divulged any of his real plans; he would have told him whatever he deemed necessary and lied to fill in the blanks. Father's true motives were always hidden.

"What are you thinking?" Danny asked. Everyone was looking at me.

The truth hit me in the form of a half remembered conversation, overheard from a doorway at my graduation party. My father's words were as clear as day:

"They are refusing to allow us to lay the pipeline through their land sir," Simon, my father's assistant, *told him.*

"I don't care what they're refusing to do, they have no rights to that land," Father replied.

Nervously Simon spoke, "Well sir, they actually do."

"Excuse me?" Father raised his voice.

"The people still technically own those lands, they never sold them."

"Simon, I'm going to lay my pipeline straight through the heart of Ogoniland whether the people like it or not."

"But sir..."

"Find me a way."

"Craig, what is the one thing Father wants above everything else?" I asked hurriedly. "What does he always tell us?"

"More land. More oil. More money. It's practically his motto."

"It *is* his motto. Ogoniland is one of the most oil rich areas in this country, and he's wanted it for years. He hasn't just heard about some attack, he's planning it. He'll force the Ogoni off their lands and lay his pipeline before they have a chance to take them back."

"How could he possibly do that?" Craig asked. "He'd need an army."

"He has one," I replied looking at Danny. "Who do we know that has the men and the weapons needed to pull something off like this, and who's willing to accept money for it?"

Danny thought for a moment, "The Captain."

I agreed, "The Captain."

An hour after my brother arrived, a helicopter landed on the outskirts of the village to take Craig away. It was dusk and the children came running wildly to see the big machine landing and taking off. Father was expecting me to be on the helicopter when it arrived in Port Harcourt, but with my refusal to leave, Craig was already fearing our Father's wrath.

Before he left Craig said, "I really wish you were getting on that helicopter with me."

"I'm sorry Craig, I really am, but I can't go with you."

"Mari please, think about what you're doing. Look at this place, look how dirty you are, and how ragged your clothes have become, this isn't you. Don't you want to come home? Don't you want to take a shower, put on clean clothes, eat a decent meal, and sleep in a real bed?"

"I can think of nothing in this world I could possibly want less. If an attack really is coming, then everyone here, all these people, are in danger, and you are asking me to abandon them. You're asking me to leave them all behind when they need me most. You want me to sell my soul to the devil for a hot shower and a plate of food. Do you really think that I can do that? Could *you* do that?"

"Of course not, that's why I'm here to get you out! I'm not leaving this country without you."

"And I'm not leaving with you."

I hugged my brother, told him I loved him, and then watched as he climbed aboard the helicopter. The wind from the propellers whipped the air and dust into a tornado. The dark machine rose above the clouds of dust, high into the sky, then shrunk into the distance towards Port Harcourt.

Danny came up beside me and wrapped an arm around my waist, "Maybe you should go, no one would blame you, and you'd be safe."

"Don't talk like that," I told him. I'm not going anywhere."

"If anything happens to you..."

"If anything happens to me, then this is exactly where I want to be. I'm not leaving you Danny, I promise."

My promise scared Danny. He wanted me to leave with my brother and, like Craig, was going to do everything in his power to change my mind. We were sitting on the ground, close to the fire, me leaning against him, when he whispered, "I'll never forgive myself if something happens to you after I had the chance to save you."

"Sending me back to that life wouldn't be saving me. I would rather die a thousand deaths here, with the people I love, than spend one more day in the same room with my father. My place is here, in this village, with Naomi and Jim, and Zack and your parents. My place is with you."

Danny did not pressure me any further, although there was more he wanted to say. He wanted to tell me to leave, to be safe, but he remained silent until I fell asleep. Danny stayed awake through the night, his mind running wild, and by the early morning he had made a plan of his own; one I never saw coming.

Danny gently eased his arm out from under Mari's head, trying his best not to wake her; she looked so peaceful in her sleep. Unable to resist, he leaned down and kissed her cheek.

"Where are you going?" She asked drowsily, barely opening her eyes to look at him.

"Shh, go back to sleep. I need to run an errand in the city, I won't be long," he answered.

Mari closed her eyes and instantly fell back to sleep. Danny took, one last look at her, hoping he was making the right choice and not some terrible mistake. He removed the keys from the truck's visor and started the engine. He drove slowly through the village occasionally waving to those rare few already awake and starting their day's work. Once he reached the main road he pressed the gas pedal down to the floor and sped towards Port Harcourt.

Danny easily located the hotel where Craig and his father were staying. He went to the most expensive hotel in the city, and parked the truck a block away in an alley where no one would notice it. Acting as if he belonged, Danny slipped by the doorman at the main entrance. He was contemplating what to do next when he saw Craig entering the lobby from the main staircase. The two boys made eye contact, and Craig motioned for Danny to meet him outside.

"What are you doing here?" Craig asked urgently, checking over his shoulder to make sure no one was following.

"I need to talk to your father," Danny said.

"Is Mari with you?"

Danny shook his head, "She doesn't know I'm here. I want to speak with your father, I think I may be able to persuade Mari to help him if he will agree to stop the attack on the villages."

"You mean, you left Mari in the village by herself?"

"Yeah..."

"Do you have any idea what you've just done?!" Craig shouted. He grabbed Danny by the arm and started pulling him down the street.

"Hey, what're you..."

"Where are you parked?"

Danny pointed, "That way, one block over. You wanna tell me what's going on?"

"Mari was right. Father ordered the attack. I overheard him on the phone an hour ago, he's given the green light for the attack." He stopped when they reached the truck. "There's something else. I heard him say: 'She's become a problem, make sure it's done.'" Craig shook Danny by the shoulders, "Do you understand what I'm telling you?! He's going to have Mari killed!"

"He can't, he needs her alive. What about the article?"

Craig shook his head, "He doesn't need her, he needs a good story for the press. Think about it, 'Mari, Murdered by Rebels' makes a good headline. He'll spin the story in his favor and no one will be the wiser."

"What do we do?"

"We have to get to her before his soldiers do. If she's rescued he'll have no choice but to bring her back to London. She'll be safe once she talks to the press, he won't dare do anything to her then. Get back to the village and get her out of there. If you go now you might beat them."

"What are you going to do?"

"I'm bringing the helicopter."

Danny threw himself into the truck. He weaved through the city traffic with no regard for pedestrians or other drivers. Old regrets resurfaced in his mind. He wasn't there to save his sister. He wasn't there when Natalie was injured. This time would be different. This time he was going to save Mari. No matter the cost.

Chapter 17

I awoke with only a hazy memory of Danny's goodbye. I had no clue what errand would have taken him away from me that morning, but he was long gone leaving me to wait for his return. The encounter with my brother troubled me. *How soon will they attack? Should I warn the rest of the village now or wait for Danny to get back?* I didn't know what to do.

"What are you thinkin' about?" Zack interrupted. All around us the village was coming to life with the sounds of people beginning what they believed to be just another ordinary day. "Are you worried about what your brother said?"

Zack's slight frame cast a shadow next to mine on the ground in front of us. I nodded and my shadow nodded with me. "You don't have to worry," he told me matter-of-factly. "If the soldiers come and burn the village again, we can always rebuild." I laughed at that and ruffled his sun-bleached hair, but it wasn't the fear of our homes burning that worried me, it was the loss of life that was certain to come with this attack.

The day was beautiful. A light breeze was blowing off the river and not a cloud could be seen for miles. The whole world felt...peaceful. The whole world except for me. Something felt wrong, deep inside me. The world was too quiet. I walked to the edge of the river and looked beyond the outskirts of the village.

Jim, sitting on the end of his boat asked, "What's wrong, Mari?"

There was something in the distance, a movement on the edge of my vision that was distinctly out of place. A wall of dust was moving and growing far past anything the small breeze could have conjured up. The source of the cloud of dust was pressing forward, moving closer to the village. Jeeps and vans. Soldiers.

"They're coming," I said quietly and then shouted again, "They're coming!"

Jim pulled my arm, "We must go now. We can hide in the jungle."

"No!" Zack ripped away from me. "I'm not leaving my parents!"

"They will know to run to the jungle, it is the safest place," Jim yelled after him, but it was too late to change the boy's mind

No sooner was Zack out of my sight than we heard the first gunshots. "We have to try to help as many as we can," my eyes pleaded with Jim.

A Rebel Star

He released me, "You are right."

"I'll see you in the jungle, my friend," I said, and then I turned and followed after Zack, into the chaos.

These men were no rebel fighters—as Danny and I had rightly guessed—they were government soldiers and they were everywhere. Armed with guns and machetes, the soldiers methodically moved through the village, setting our homes on fire and murdering those who got in their way. Thick, black smoke rose high into the air. People ran to the river banks to escape it and were met by more soldiers coming in on boats that landed on the shores; their gunfire silenced the people's screams.

I arrived at the center of the village in the peak of the chaos. I could do nothing for the people who had been trapped there—the ones who had been waiting patiently in line for their daily supply of water. I ran past them all, tears burning my eyes, either from the heavy smoke or the horror of the scene before me I wasn't quite sure. Although I tried my best to help others, shouting at them to run towards the jungle, finding Zack was my priority.

I heard a small child screaming ahead of me, her cries coming from inside a burning hut. I needed to keep moving, but how could I leave? Taking a deep breath and, pulling my shirt over my nose and mouth, I entered the hut. The roof was on fire and I could see nothing through all the smoke. It took me one whole, precious minute to get my bearings and find the little girl. I picked her up and quickly ran back outside. There was no time to go searching for her family, so I carried her with me as I ran through the village.

"Mari!" Someone shouted my name. Natalie was alone and running towards me.

"I have to find Zack!" I yelled. When she was closer I said, "Here, take the girl." Natalie offered her arm and I dropped the child into it.

"I've got her," Natalie said. "Mari, come with me, you'll never find the boy in this."

I shook my head, "I can't leave him. I'll be right behind you."

She argued no further and joined the few others running towards the jungle. As I ran, closing the gap between myself and Danny's home, I found myself wishing beyond all hope that no one would be there, that they would be long gone, in the jungle with all the others. What I found instead, I will never forget. I could see figures, distorted by the smoke, in the field next to the hut. I moved closer, checking over my shoulder to make sure no one was following. I moved slowly, some inner part of me knowing I did not want to see what was in the field.

Tess and Barry's home was blazing with bright orange flames. I shielded my face with my arm as I passed by it. I reluctantly moved forward until the figures became clearer. Zack's lean silhouette was kneeling on the ground, his parents' bodies lying in front of him.

"Zack," I called his name. He didn't turn. I reached out and turned his head away, covering his eyes so he could no longer see his parents' bodies. Tess and Barry were face down in the dirt, bullet casings on the ground all around them. There was no time for me to look more closely, it was too late for them, and we needed to get out of the village. "Come on Zack, we need to go."

I pulled him to his feet. He was completely in shock, so I grabbed his hand and dragged him behind me as we took the quickest path to the jungle: back through the center of the village, into the heart of the attack. A thousand questions raced through my mind as we pressed forward: Where were Naomi and Jim?

Had they made it to the jungle or were they still in the village? What about Danny? I knew he was in the city far from any danger, but what if he came back? He could be killed trying to find us. I shook the thought away.

The center of our village had been transformed. No longer was it a peaceful place for gathering or chatting with friends and neighbors, or collecting the fresh water needed for our survival. It was a war zone. Bodies littered the pathways, their blood pooling in the orange dust. The villagers were slaughtered no differently than the cows in the market. There was no use in trying to block the images from Zack's eyes; no matter where we turned there was another of our neighbors lying dead on the ground. The boy followed my lead without making a single sound, his young mind soaking up all of the horrors surrounding us. We kept as close as we could to the burning huts, using the smoke as cover. The soldiers were everywhere, coming from all directions, pouring into the village and outnumbering us all.

"We're not gonna make it," Zack finally spoke.

"Yes we are," I replied sternly, though I wasn't sure I believed it myself. The split second that I stopped scanning the paths around us to reply to him, was when we were finally spotted. A soldier came from the path to our left and threw me to the ground with Zack, the three of us landing in a human knot. The wind was knocked out of me and I could not get my bearings. Zack regained his footing first and I felt him grab my arm and try to pull me away. The soldier pulled harder, keeping me on the ground.

"Go!" I shouted at Zack. "Get out of here! Get to the jungle!"

The soldier was on top of me, his legs straddling my torso, a large, rusted machete in his hand. I kicked and punched but the soldier was too strong for me. He raised his arm high, the machete's shadow falling over my face. I closed my eyes and waited for the blade to fall. The soldier cried out and I saw Zack pulling on his arm. No, he wasn't pulling, he was biting. Zack was biting the arm holding the machete, giving me a chance to break free. I pushed and pulled but he held me tight. Even with the two of us fighting, I was still trapped beneath him. The soldier punched Zack with his free arm, hitting him in the face. Zack fell backwards, dazed and defeated. The soldier raised the machete again, anger and hatred filled his pitch black eyes. He swung his arm in a downward arc, aiming for my head.

"NO!" I heard Zack scream. Then everything was quiet.

The machete was laying on the ground next to my head, and the soldier was lying on top of me, his body limp. I rolled his body off of me; my hands becoming sticky with his blood. The soldiers back was riddled with bullets. Another soldier was standing in front of us, his gun pointed in our direction. He wasn't like the other soldiers. His uniform was different, his skin fair, and his clear blue eyes showed no signs of hatred. He lowered his gun and I knew, not only that he would not kill us, but that he was the one who saved me.

"Thank you," I mouthed the words to him. He tilted his head down into a nod, then turned and disappeared back into the chaos.

We started running again. The closer we got to the end of the village the less we worried about being seen. We were running for our lives with no time to look for cover. We were careless and almost paid for it when a soldier leaped out in front of us, blocking our way. I recognized him immediately as the corrupt captain that I bribed to save Zack in the market, the one who killed Danny's sister and the old man at the road block, the same one who shot Natalie in her arm, and the leader of this attack.

"You," he snarled baring his crooked teeth. His laugh echoed through my ears, "You will not escape me again."

I pushed Zack behind me as the Captain lifted his gun. *This is it,* I thought. After everything I went through I was going to die by the hand of the most corrupt official in Nigeria. There was nowhere for me to run, no way for me to fight him, it was just me and him and the gun between us. My eyes never left his as I waited for him to pull the trigger. The sound of gunfire came from behind us, missing me and Zack by inches, and slamming into the Captain. Danny was standing there with a weapon he must have stolen from one of the dead soldiers. The Captain fell to the ground, choking on his own blood. Danny approached and stood over him, not a word passed from his lips as he watched his enemy die. With a sputtering noise the Captain released his final breath and died at our feet.

Danny reached his hand out for me and without a second's hesitation I took it.

"Let's go!" He yelled, and together the three of us ran.

We took cover behind one of the huts as we reached the outskirts of the village. There was a long stretch of open space between us and the safety of the jungle. Danny surveyed the scene, planning a way for us to safely cross our own version of "no man's land." He seemed to be waiting for something.

"What took you so long?" I joked, but Danny didn't laugh.

He furrowed his brow and asked, "Are you okay?" His eyes were inspecting me and I remembered I was covered in the solder's blood.

"It's not my blood," I told him.

"This is," he said gently touching the side of my head. I must have bumped it when the soldier knocked me down, but I felt nothing.

"I'm fine. What are we waiting for? We need to get into the jungle, it's where everyone went."

"Mari, listen to me..." Danny was cut off by gunfire. The soldiers were closing in, if we didn't move soon we weren't going to make it. We crouched lower to make ourselves smaller targets. "We're going to be okay. I'm not going to let anything happen to you, but I need you to trust me. Mari, do you trust me?"

"Of course I do. What are you thinking?"

As if in answer to my question the wind picked up, throwing dust against us, and a loud, whirring noise filled the air. A helicopter! The helicopter that had picked up my brother the night before, landed in the clearing between us and the jungle. I was so relieved; we were saved! The three of us could get onto the helicopter and be air lifted to safety. We could regroup then go in search of other survivors. Everything would be okay, at least that's what I thought before I looked at Danny's face.

"Danny, please tell me you're getting on that helicopter with me," I shouted above the roar of the helicopter. The gunfire had ceased, the soldiers recognizing that the helicopter belonged to my father.

Danny ignored me and spoke to Zack, "I need you to run for the jungle right now before that 'copter leaves. The soldiers will only hold fire for so long. Go find the others."

"What about you?" Zack asked alarmed.

"I'll be right behind you, now go!"

Zack looked at the two of us one last time, then took off running. None of the soldiers fired at him and we watched as he safely disappeared behind the trees. My brother emerged from the helicopter and waved me forward.

"I'm not leaving without you," I told Danny.

"Mari, you have to get out of this place, it's not safe for you anymore."

"I don't care!"

"Mari! Stop arguing and listen to me. You were always meant to leave. You have to go back and tell people what you've seen here. You're the only one with the power to help us!"

"I promised I would never leave you!"

He leaned in closer. "You're not leaving me." He took my hand and I felt him place something around my wrist. It was his sister's bracelet, the one he wore every day since her death, the one he accidentally gave to me the night we stayed in the rebel camp, which I returned to him at Agbokim Falls when he told me its history.

I began to cry, "No, I can't."

"Go to London. Be safe. Tell people the truth about this place and I promise you we *will* see each other again." Danny pulled me to him and kissed me quickly on the lips. "I love you, Mari."

"And I love you."

It was the first time either of us had said the words. For a brief moment it felt like the world around us had stopped. I knew deep down and with all my heart that those words were true. I loved Danny more than anything or anyone else in the world and I knew that I would see him again. "I'll come back for you," I swore to him in our last moment. "I'll find a way to expose my father and the company, then I'm coming home!"

Craig was shouting my name. He pulled me away from Danny, stealing our last precious second together, and pushed me towards the helicopter. The soldiers began firing again. A sharp pain, at first like a punch that nearly threw me off balance, hit me in my left shoulder. Blood ran down the front of my shirt and this time it was definitely my own. Adrenaline and my brother pushed me forward until I toppled onto the floor of the helicopter.

Craig jumped in beside me and shouted, "Go, go, go!"

I watched the ground and the remnants of my village below us. I could still see Danny. He was surrounded by soldiers, his arms raised high into the air, his gun lying at his feet. One of the soldiers punched him in the stomach and he doubled over. Two more soldiers took him by the arms and began to drag him away.

"No!" I was screaming, but the sound of my voice was lost over the roar of the helicopter. The village was nothing but black smoke and orange flames. There were still a few people staggering towards the jungle, but the soldiers were right behind them. The soldiers lined up, took aim, and mowed down what was left of the villagers. I screamed at my brother and the pilot, and cried until the tears blurred my vision.

I blacked out on the floor of the helicopter, in my brother's arms.

Chapter 18

Somewhere between arriving in Port Harcourt, finding the Ogoni villages, meeting a famous writer and a rebel leader, learning the truth about my mother, falling in love and then losing it all, I turned 18. After everything I went through and everything I learned, nothing seemed more insignificant than a missed birthday, except it was that missed birthday that had at last set me free. I was 18 and legally could no longer be compelled to do anything for my father. Legally I was free; physically I was trapped. Two weeks after being air lifted from the village, I was safely tucked away in my London bedroom, healing from a gunshot wound to the shoulder. Images of burning huts, people fleeing, and soldiers... and Danny, haunted me. Sleep eluded me and nothing could ease my mind. I awoke screaming every night which forced Ruth to move into my bedroom. She held me like I was a child until I calmed down and slept on the floor next to my bed every night. I spoke to no one and ate next to nothing. I refused all medications, pain killers, and doctor's visits, choosing instead to remain in my bed, under the covers, hidden from the world, and haunted by my thoughts.

After a month of what Ruth called *disturbing behavior*, she declared, "Enough!" Throwing open my curtains to let the light in, she dragged me out of my bed and into a hot bath. Ignoring my protests she lathered and scrubbed shampoo into my hair and pressed my head below the water to rinse it out.

"Ow!" I sputtered as I sat up. The hot water burned my wound.

"You'll live girl. Do you hear me? You'll live."
And I realized she was talking about more than the hole
in my shoulder.

Ruth dressed me and helped me down the stairs
to the kitchen where Joseph made me something to eat.
Gradually my body began to heal. In the days that
followed I took my medications and ate my food, but
there was nothing that could stop my nightmares.

Father kept his distance for as long as he could
until it was finally time for me to live up to my end of
the deal. "You have an interview with Michael P.
tomorrow afternoon," he informed me one day. I was
sitting alone in the den.

"And if I refuse?"

He put his face close to mine, "If you refuse, or
if the article is not to my liking, I will make sure that
whatever friends you have left in this world will be
taken from you."

Instinctively my eyes drifted towards the kitchen where Ruth and Joseph were preparing our dinner. My father chuckled, "Not just them, Mari. I mean that I will destroy everyone you love if you even think of betraying me."

"You've already taken everyone that I love."

"Not quite everyone," he leaned closer and spoke in my ear. "Your people are alive in a refugee camp, and I am holding your boyfriend prisoner. One wrong move and I'll order their executions." Father straightened and turned to leave.

"Like you ordered Mother's?" I called after him.

He stiffened, "I really must start giving you more credit, Mari." He tapped the side of his nose with a single finger, "Now you know what happens to those who get in my way."

★◆★

"Mari! I cannot tell you how thrilled I am to see you! Come in, come in, sit down. Would you like some tea?" Michael P. was exactly how I remembered him; warm and friendly, with a happy spirit that reminded me of Danny's father, it brought tears to my eyes.

"My dear, whatever is the matter?" Deeply concerned, Michael moved to the identical black, leather chair next to mine and offered me a tissue. We were in his downtown office, the door sealing us off from the bustling news office below. Only the most senior staff members of the paper were allowed offices on the second floor and Michael had certainly earned his right to one over the years. It was true that he wrote mostly gossip, but his column held weight among London's social class. If Michael didn't like you, then London didn't either. Some even dared to call him one of the most influential, if not powerful, men in the city, placing him in the same league as my father.

"I'm alright," I assured him, waving the tissue away. "Michael, my father arranged this meeting so I could tell you the story of how he saved me from rebel fighters in Nigeria."

"And that is not what you're going to tell me, is it?"

"No. I'm going to tell you the truth."

"Which is?"

"My father is a murderer."

★◆★

"Mari, I cannot print this story and you are well aware of that." Michael was calmly sitting back in his chair mulling over my account.

"But you must believe me," I replied.

391

"I admit I've always had my suspicions about Lila's death, though I never could imagine why he would have wanted her dead. Your story has shed some light on my old theories, and I am grateful to at last have answers, but one would have to be completely mad to present your allegations to the editors for printing, and I am *not* completely mad. Though I think my wife may not always agree," he laughed at his own joke.

"How could you *not* want to print this? I've told you that my father, one of London's richest and arguably most powerful men, murdered his wife, and you're not going to print it? You're a journalist, I thought your job was to expose people like him."

"My job is to print the truth in a factual way that has evidentiary support. There is no proof that what you said here today is true."

"He admitted it clear as day to me!"

"And he will claim that he did not. He will say that you are suffering from a form of post-traumatic stress based on your recent horrifying experiences in Nigeria."

"So he's going to get away with it then?"

"He's already gotten away with it for the last sixteen years. You won't bring your father down with charges of murder. It will never happen."

I leaned forward in my chair, "Then *how* do I take him down?"

Michael sighed, "You're determined to do this?"

"With every fiber of my being."

"Have you considered the cost? And I don't mean only your share of it. You told me he is holding your boyfriend..."

"Danny," I interrupted.

"Right, Danny. He threatened Danny and the rest of the Ogoni people in the refugee camps, and don't forget about your friends Ruth and Joseph who live here under his careful watch. And what about your brother? What will happen to him if you succeed? If you are going to take on your father then you cannot do it blindly, you *have* to have a plan."

"Then help me make one. Tell me what I need to do Michael and I'll do it."

Michael stood and walked to the large window beside his desk, his hands clasped behind his back. He was silent for several minutes and I waited as patiently as I could for him to speak. I was fully aware that what I was asking him to do would change his life forever, the way that my life had already changed. I was asking him to risk his life and the safety of his family, which I had no right to do. Without his help, though, I didn't know what I was going to do.

"Please Michael," I begged. "Tell me what I need."

There was a long pause before he responded, "You need proof."

"What kind of proof?"

"Your father, like all rich men, has one weakness," Michael told me.

"Which is?"

"His money. It is what buys him his power, without it he has nothing. He uses it to buy himself protection. He pays men to turn a blind eye to his bad business dealings. He greases the palms of important men everywhere he goes. Money is what makes him the man that he is and the second anyone gets in the way of his making more he destroys them. But, money leaves a trail and we need to follow it."

"And how exactly do we do that?"

"We need an accountant."

★◆★

The particular accountant Michael P. had in mind was one who had worked for my father for over twenty years. His name was Eddie and though he was the best accountant in London he was also a radical, always joining the ranks of some cause which never stood a chance of winning, but which always seemed to make him ineligible for any type of promotion. He worked tirelessly to earn his substantial income, but had become a prisoner in his own world. No other company would hire him, Father made sure of that, and whenever the notion of leaving the oil company came over him Father was there to remind him of his lack of options. Eddie had been bullied as a boy in school. He was teased as a young man in University. He was persecuted for his politics in the years after that and he was kept under my father's thumb, forced to do his bidding for nearly all of his adult life. In other words, Eddie was fed up.

I knew Eddie fairly well, so when Michael mentioned his name I was angry at myself for not thinking of him sooner. Michael wrote Eddie's address on a slip of paper and told me to go straight to his house when I left the office.

"I'll call him to let him know you're on your way," Michael told me. "You can trust Eddie. I've known him for many years, he will not betray you; but tell your story to no one except Eddie. No one can know what we're trying to do, especially your father. You're going to have to play along with him for now; do you think you can do that?"

I nodded, "What about your article? Father is expecting one."

Michael sat down comfortably behind his desk and cracked his knuckles, "Oh I'm sure my creative writing skills are up to the task."

Eddie lived in a modest home considering the salary he earned working for the oil company. His house was small and decorated in a way only a man can decorate. Large pieces of dark furniture crowded the living area and the hallways, giving me a sense of claustrophobia. I followed him down one of the hallways into the only room that ever mattered to Eddie: the library. Books stood in towering stacks, some as tall as me, and covered every inch of the room. Old bound volumes of encyclopedias, classic novels, some first editions, and even some modern novels numbered among the many. There were more books than a person could possibly count, but I was sure Eddie knew how many and where exactly to find each one.

He sat down on a sofa and motioned for me to join him. An open novel lay face down on the table as though I'd interrupted him in the middle of his afternoon reading. He looked comfortable, as one would expect to look in their own home, wearing a light blue shirt unbuttoned at the neck, with the sleeves rolled up, and a loose pair of khaki pants. He was barefoot with his legs crossed, carefully studying me.

"I don't normally invite people into my home," he stated. "I never imagined I'd entertain someone like you here, but Michael has vouched for you and I trust him."

"Michael said that you would be able help me."

"That depends on what you need help with. Michael told me nothing about why you're here, perhaps you could enlighten me."

"I'm looking for evidence that can back me up for claims I am making against my father and the oil company. I want to expose them for the murderous cheats they are, once and for all. And, before you call me absolutely mad or ask me if I've thought this all the way through, let me assure you: I have. I have weighed each of my options very carefully and have come to the conclusion that I *must* see this through no matter the cost or consequences because it is the right thing to do.

The trouble is, I can't do this on my own. Michael has agreed to print my story, but only if I can provide the evidence to back it up, which is where you come in."

Eddie wasted no time in replying, "You are young, a bit naïve or completely foolish, I can't decide which, and absolutely mad." He paused. "So when do we start?"

Three hours later, with my story finished, and a well consumed tray of tea and biscuits on the table between us, Eddie and I agreed upon the best way to proceed.

"Michael's instincts are right, we need to follow the money your father is using to buy off the soldiers and government officials. It won't be easy, your father will have been very careful, but there is never a way to move large amounts of money without leaving a trail. A thorough audit on all the accounts should reveal the truth. It's a long process, but I might be able to finish quicker if you can narrow down the dates for me."

"I can do that," I replied.

"It will take time Mari, it's important you understand that. This game that we are playing is dangerous and will not be over quickly, it may even take years before we are finished! There is no guarantee either of us will be there when it ends. I'm not going to ask if you're sure you want to do this, I can see that you are; but at least let an old man experienced in these matters offer you some advice. It does not matter who you are or what you are fighting for, there are sacrifices for every cause that have to be made along the way. Some of those sacrifices will be small and easy to live with, but there are others that will feel unbearable. If there is any chance of this succeeding then you will have to find a way to keep pressing forward, even when it seems impossible. I won't insult you by asking if you're truly ready to do that, I was young once and I know what your answer will be; but promise me that you will give my words serious consideration before you take any further steps in this endeavor." He thrust his hand forward and I accepted it.

"I will. Thank you for your time Eddie, I will contact you soon."

Chapter 19

A Star Returns

By Michael P.

After months of worrying and unanswered questions as to the well-being of my favorite socialite, I have at last received the good news that Marienela is alive and well. More than that she has returned to us with tales both horrifying and fascinating. She has privileged me with the exclusive right to share our private interview with all of you. In her very own words, her story is as follows:

<u>Michael</u>: Mari, I'm not sure if you've seen my last article concerning you or not, but all of us have been wondering...where on earth have you been?

<u>Mari</u>: I did see your article, Michael, and am very thankful to know how concerned everyone was for me. It is good to know that if I am ever truly missing that someone would care enough to come looking for me. In answer to your question, I secretly travelled to Nigeria, more specifically the Niger River Delta.

<u>Michael</u>: What was it that made you decide to go there?

<u>Mari</u>: Well, as I'm sure you know, my father conducts a large portion of his business in Nigeria. What most people don't know, however, is that my mother was living there when they met. She grew up in Nigeria and one of her dying wishes was that one day I would see where she came from. My father agreed to let me

travel alone, and so I left without telling anyone else where I was going. I felt that this was a journey that I needed to take on my own, and I'm very glad that I did.

Michael: So, tell me everything. What did you see and do? You were gone a very long time.

Mari: I spent a couple of weeks in the city of Port Harcourt, which is like the beating heart of the Niger River Delta. The city is large and teeming with people. The Borikiri street market is the largest, busiest market I've ever seen in my life. There were people everywhere selling every different kind of foods and goods that you could imagine. After that I travelled with a guide to the village where my mother grew up, and discovered that many of the older ones still remembered her. The woman she had considered a sister invited me to stay in the village, so I did. It was a rewarding experience to live among the Ogoni people, though I must say that I missed home very much, especially indoor plumbing.

Michael: You mean there was no running water?

Mari: There was a single water pump in the middle of the village that everyone shared and that was it.

Michael: And you lived like that for several months?!

Mari: Well the Ogoni live that way every day. As I said before, the experience was rewarding and put my life in perspective, I wouldn't trade it for anything; but still, having said that, I am very glad to be back.

Michael: I imagine so! Now I must ask you this, I see that you are wearing a sling around your arm from some kind of injury. Would you tell me what happened to you?

Mari: Unfortunately, although the country is one of the most beautiful in the world, there are many issues with its government and people. There are many rebel groups located throughout the River Delta and thankfully my father received information that one of those groups was planning to attack some of the *villages in the area and he arrived just in time to rescue me. I was caught in the middle of the village during the rebels' attack, but my father was able to send a helicopter to get me. As I was running to the helicopter I was shot in the shoulder. It's taken some time to heal, but I am at last feeling better.*

<u>Michael</u>: I am so glad to hear it!

Marienela means 'Rebel Star,' she told me. Isn't that a fitting title for one so brave? I think so. Our dear Mari has travelled far and experienced more than many of us could possibly imagine and although she has changed, it is for the better. I am sure I speak for all my readers when I say, "Welcome home Mari! We have missed you!"

"You most certainly do *not* speak for all of your readers," Kirstin slammed her newspaper down in a most unlady-like fashion, rattling the teacups in their saucers. She couldn't see me approaching our usual table at the Ritz with her back facing the entrance. Michael's article had done the trick, pleasing my father and removing suspicion from our secret plans. Michael's lies spread like wildfire throughout London, and perhaps even further. Our phone rang for hours daily; other reporters begged to interview me, but I refused them all having already done enough to appease my father. I tried hiding away in our home, but Father insisted that I be more social and show my face in public. He needed the press to see me acting normally and what could be more normal than afternoon tea with my oldest friend, Kirstin, and my former boyfriend, Brian, who by the way, had begun dating in my absence?

Craig, there for me as always, agreed to be my companion and, with my good arm looped through his, guided me over to our table at the exact moment of Kirstin's outburst. She blushed in embarrassment as soon as she saw us and immediately tried to fix her mistake.

"Mari! It's so good to see you again, I was just telling Brian..."

I held up my hand to silence her as I settled into my seat. "Please Kirstin, there's no need for you to defend yourself. You and I were always friends on the surface, but it was never a secret that we were always rivaling against each other. A lot has changed since I left so can we agree that the games are at last over, and maybe give our friendship a real try this time?"

My words caught all three in our little party off guard, but none as much as Kirstin herself. She was struggling to find the right response until her face finally softened and she replied, "I think that might be nice."

"I was told the two of you have started dating," I said looking at my ex, Brian, whose proposal ultimately led me to leave for Nigeria, and then at Kirstin. "I think that's great." I smiled and took a sip of the hot tea. I heard Brian release the breath he had been holding, and the overall mood at the table lightened.

With everyone's feelings out in the open, the rest of our afternoon went smoothly. I quietly listened as Kirstin and the boys chatted away, trying their best to fill me in on all the gossip I missed. I smiled and gasped in all the appropriate places, but my heart wasn't in it and in the end I think they could tell. I couldn't keep my thoughts away from Eddie searching tirelessly through his records for the small bit of proof that would change everything, or from the thought of the Ogoni living in the terrible conditions of the refugee camp. Over the weeks, using Michael's various contacts in both London and Nigeria, I located the camp where they were being held. What I was told was not comforting. People died in the camp every day. There was little food, barely any shelter, and diseases were spreading as quickly as could be expected when so many people are forced to live so close together. I was assured there were soldiers posted all along the perimeter of the camp to protect the people from any further attack, but I could hear the underlying truth to those words: no one was leaving the camp. I was certain that any person caught trying to leave would be killed and considered one less mouth to feed. I needed to find a way to free the people inside those fences and I needed to find it fast.

A part of me hoped Naomi, Jim, and Zack were not in the camp but safely hidden somewhere in the jungle. I also knew that the dangers of them being caught by soldiers outside the camp far outweighed the dangers of being trapped within. Either way I knew at least there was a chance of me finding them. Danny, however, was a different story. Father was holding him captive, but where on earth would I begin to look? There was an obvious and common solution to both of these problems, all I needed to do was make one more phone call.

When we were finished with tea, I suggested the four of us go for a walk; the day was so beautiful I felt like being outside. I had an appointment scheduled with Eddie for later that afternoon and was going to have to find a way to quietly escape from the house later without raising suspicion. We walked through the same park as we did all those months ago, before I left, when I was a different person and Brian had proposed. I was surprised when he offered me his arm as we approached the very spot of that proposal. We stood on the bridge leaning on the railing, watching our reflections in the water below us.

"You're different," Brian remarked.

"I feel different," I replied. "I'm glad things seem to have worked out for you, Brian."

"I think you were right, you and I getting married would have been a mistake. Sure, we would have made a great alliance and we would have been fine, but neither of us would have been happy."

"And are you? Happy, I mean?"

He smiled to himself, "Yes, I think I am."

I nudged his shoulder with mine, "Then I'm glad."

"What about you? I mean what will you do now?"

"Oh don't you worry about me," I grinned. "I have plans."

★◆★

"You handled that maturely," my brother commented later as our driver took us home. "You've changed a lot. I'm proud of you."

"Thank you for coming with me. I'm not sure it would've gone as smoothly without you." I reached over and squeezed his hand.

"Anytime, little sister, anytime."

"Craig?"

"Yes?"

"I really missed you while I was gone."

He smiled, "I really missed you too."

"I never thanked you for saving me."

"You know you don't have to, Mari..."

"I know. Only, I guess I've realized that I don't say it often enough, and you've always been an amazing brother, and I wanted you to know that I appreciate you always being there for me so...thank you."

"Is everything okay?" Craig asked. "The last time you acted this strangely you disappeared for months without a word."

"I know, I'm really sorry I did that to you. I wasn't thinking."

"Just do me a favor, promise me the next time you're about to do something crazy, you'll warn me first."

I bit my bottom lip and considered. *Should I tell him what my plans are? I'm not even sure that they're going to work yet and he could try to stop me.*

Reading my thoughts, Craig asked, "You're already planning something aren't you?"

"Yes," I could at least say that much.

"Are you going to tell me what it is?"

I shook my head, "Not yet."

Craig rolled his eyes and let out and exasperated sigh. He leaned his head back against the car seat and closed his eyes. "And when should I be expecting to hear about this latest scheme?"

"Soon," I replied. "Very soon."

End of Book One

Bibliography

1. Saro-Wiwa, Ken. <u>A Month and a Day: A Detention Diary</u>. Harmondsworth, Middlesex: England, 1995. Print. Speech entitled *Before the Curtain Falls*, written and delivered by Ken Saro-Wiwa on October 10, 1991. Pages 82-87.

2. Quote taken from the official website for the Movement of the Survival of the Ogoni People. <u>www.mosop.org</u>. Copyright © 2009-2015 Movement of the Survival of the Ogoni People (MOSOP). All rights reserved.

3. Poem written by Ken Saro-Wiwa for the first official Ogoni Day. January 4, 1993. Quote taken from the official website for the Movement of the Survival of the Ogoni People. <u>www.mosop.org</u>. Copyright © 2009-2015 Movement of the Survival of the Ogoni People (MOSOP). All rights reserved.

Alyssa Rae was born in Massachusetts and currently resides in a historic town in North Carolina. She is a devoted and enthusiastic reader, writer, and movie goer. Her debut novel, *A Lion's Pride*, was published in early 2013. *A Rebel Star* is her second novel with many more projects soon to follow. Stay tuned...

Visit the author's website: www.alyssarae.com